SUBMITTING TO THE CATTLEMAN

Cowboy Doms, Book Six

BJ WANE

Published by Blushing Books
An Imprint of
ABCD Graphics and Design, Inc.
A Virginia Corporation
977 Seminole Trail #233
Charlottesville, VA 22901

BJ Wane
Submitting to the Cattleman

EBook ISBN: 978-1-64563-146-0
Print ISBN: 978-1-64563-168-2
v1

Chapter 1

The end of August

Are you sure I can't walk you out to your car?"

Leslie Collins smiled at her fellow teacher as the rest of their group said their goodbyes. Shaking her head, she wished she could return the interest in Alan Colwich's hazel eyes, but where had wishing ever gotten her? "Thanks, Alan, but I've already ordered another drink. You go on and I'll see you Monday." She prayed he wouldn't insist on staying until she was ready to leave the club. As much as she dreaded returning to her apartment to spend another night, and weekend alone, it would be worse if he asked her out again or she had to sit here for another hour making small talk while trying not to notice his 'puppy dog' looks.

Alan hesitated and Leslie held her breath until he nodded and stood. "If you're sure then I'll head out. See you Monday." After dropping a tip on the table, he waved and she breathed a sigh of relief watching him wind his way through the tables in the dim interior.

A heavy weight of despair pressed against her chest. Doing

the right thing almost four years ago had cost her everything and left her future in limbo. She'd been coping with her distraught circumstances fairly well until recently. Her mind drifted to another club, one where she'd discovered a satisfying distraction that helped her get through the long, lonely days and even longer, lonelier nights, or so she'd thought. Tomorrow would mark the third Saturday she wouldn't make the thirty-minute drive from Billings to the private BDSM club, The Barn, and she missed what she'd found there.

"Thank you." Leslie smiled at the young waitress who delivered her gin and tonic, remembering her stint serving drinks as she'd worked her way through college.

Too bad her higher education hadn't offered a class on how to cope after testifying in a murder case where the defendant's father vowed retribution. Being in the wrong place at the wrong time sucked. She'd tried to keep from forming close friendships with her co-workers and the club members at The Barn, knowing a relationship of any kind could have no future and might even put someone else at risk if her identity in the witness protection program were discovered.

Keeping herself isolated had been the hardest part about accepting her fate when the threats against her had escalated to a drive by shooting at her house. She'd been enjoying a friendly visit from the older widower next door when he'd opened her front door just as several bullets pelted the front porch. He'd recovered from a shoulder wound, but the incident scared her enough to convince her to accept the offer of relocation.

Leslie sipped her drink as she gazed around the quiet bar, the low hum of conversation and faint music strains reaching her secluded corner table. With the exception of the lone, dark haired man with broad shoulders seated at the bar, everyone had someone to spend the Friday night with, maybe even the weekend or longer. God, she missed the nights at The Barn, the relief from the stress and despondency of her solitary life she could attain by indulging in a long scene with an attentive Dom. The limited relationships with both the Masters and the other submissive members had been enough to sustain her since joining the private club three years ago, but that was before witnessing the blissful happiness of several members committing to the one person who could fulfill all their needs.

No, Leslie thought, taking another long drink, it was easier to stay away than return and spend an evening pretending she was happy for those who were free to enjoy everything life, and the right person had to offer. The Doms she'd scened with were good to her, but not one ever looked at her the way the newly committed Masters gazed at their wives. The hardest relationship to accept had been Nan's recent commitment to Master Dan, the two long-time members and friends having made that choice a week or two before she'd stopped attending. To make matters even worse, she couldn't risk a casual night of sex with a friend like Alan without getting his hopes up that it would lead to something more, and she refused to use him that way.

Leslie should have known by now wallowing in self-pity never helped. She took a moment to eye the man at the bar again, this time catching a glimpse of his rugged profile beneath the black Stetson, a straight nose and the sardonic curl of one side of his mouth as a young woman approached him. His reply to whatever come-on she whispered in his ear sent her trouncing off in a huff. Leslie wondered how low her spirits would have to sink before she approached a stranger with a needy proposition. Maybe, if one look stirred her juices the same as eying that man, she wouldn't mind the rash, desperate act so much. If nothing else, a night indulging in sex with a stranger would alleviate the loneliness for a short time, give her something else to think about.

By the time she downed two more drinks, stood to leave and the room spun around her, she realized she should have paid more attention to her alcohol intake. *I can do this as long as I go slow.* Since she wasn't about to call one of her co-workers to drive her the few blocks back home, she forced herself to walk a straight path toward the door. She made it with only one stumble and as she breathed in the warm summer air, her woozy senses calmed a bit.

At least, Leslie thought her head had cleared enough to drive until she teetered through the well-lit parking lot in search of her car and rammed her hip into the bumper of a massive pickup truck. Swearing under her breath, she pushed away and wobbled toward the sidewalk she could follow straight to her apartment door. With her inebriated head bemoaning the return to her lonely apartment she never heard or saw the punk purse snatcher sneak up behind her until he tried pulling her bag from her grasp.

"Hey!" she cried out with a desperate tug to keep hold of her purse. "Leave me alone!" Tears welled as frustration over everything shook her.

The kid, who looked all of sixteen, took umbrage of Leslie daring to fight back and stunned her further with a back-handed swing that landed her on the concrete with a jarring thud and red-hot pain blossoming across her cheek. Reeling from both the dizzying fall and the blow, she had to blink several times and shake her head to make sense of the angry shout and large man now grappling with her assailant. Big men wearing cowboy hats, denim and boots were a dime a dozen in Montana, but no one had ever come to her rescue before. Her aching heart rolled over in appreciation even before he turned concerned eyes on her as the wily teenager broke from his hold, giving up her purse before taking off.

"Fucking kid," he swore, squatting down in front of her. His rough voice sent tingles of awareness dancing down her spine, the intent look in his dark eyes reminding her of the observant gazes of the Doms at the club. He thumbed his hat back far enough for her to make out his rugged features and the dark shadow of his five o'clock beard in the meager amber glow of the streetlight and realize he was the same man she had ogled in the bar. "You okay, sweetheart?"

"I, yes, I think so." He helped Leslie up and the street whipped around her in staggering circles. "Whoa," she gasped, grabbing onto his thick forearm, the muscles rippling under her hands as he wrapped his other arm around her waist.

"This is where too much alcohol will land you. Come on, I'll drive you home."

His firm, no-nonsense tone calmed Leslie's racing heartbeat even if she didn't care for his lecture any more than she wanted to spend another long night alone. God, it felt good to lean on someone for a change, not to mention the warm rush spreading through her body from his firm hold and take-charge manner. She must be either really drunk or really desperate for relief if a stranger's kindness was tugging on her neglected needs as a sexual submissive.

"My car's in the parking lot behind us and I live just a few blocks away." Whether because of the scare she'd just experienced or from her self-pitying melancholy mood of late, she didn't want him to walk away yet. If that made her a pathetic mess, she didn't care and relief swept through her shaken body when he tightened his arm around her waist.

"I can't let you drive in your condition." He ran calloused fingertips over her puffy cheek, a light caress she felt clear to her toes. "You need something on this, and learning to duck wouldn't hurt. I'll give you two choices. Call a friend to come get you or let me take you home. We can return to the bar and let the bartender know where you're going and with whom, to ease your mind. I'd say you need to report this, but the odds of finding that kid aren't likely."

Leslie didn't hear much after he offered to see her home. Was it stupid to let a stranger know where she lived? Oh, yeah, but not as dumb as wishing he would stay and exert some of that commanding attitude in a different way. She craved a distraction from her isolated life and the bleak future looming ahead of her, and spending more time with this panty-dampening stranger worked for her.

"I think," she whispered, swaying closer to that rock-hard body, "I can trust someone who was nice enough to come to my rescue."

He shook his head, his mouth turning down in a frown that drew a shiver. "We will go talk to the bartender and then I'll drive you home. You've had too much to drink to make a rational decision."

"How do you know how much I drank tonight?" she grumbled, stumbling alongside him as he steered her toward the bar.

"Because I saw you. You drank three drinks *after* I arrived and I'm guessing at least one before I spotted you in the corner with your friends. One of them should have stayed to see you home."

The censure lacing his voice was unfair to Alan since he had offered to come back to her apartment, but she was too pleased he had noticed her to argue with him. He kept hold of her hand as they returned to the bar. Even in heels, Leslie's head only came to those wide shoulders, his towering height making her appear shorter than five foot six. She always did prefer big men, like the Masters at the club. Her throat tightened as she thought of them again, and their recent commitments. Staying away these past weeks failed to put what was missing, and always would be, from her life out of her mind.

"Okay, let's get you home."

Leslie shook her head, trying to clear the fog as she watched him return his wallet to his back pocket after speaking with the bartender, figuring he'd shown proof of his identity.

"So, you two decided I was safe with you, is that it?" The breathless catch in her voice could have been attributed to the quick tug on her hand and the spinning room as he led her back outside, but she knew that wasn't it. The submissive part of her psyche reveled in his take charge manner, just as she knew come morning and sobriety she would likely regret her actions tonight.

"Since I already know you're safe with me, I was hoping to ease your mind." He looked at her as he opened the passenger door to the massive truck she had bumped into earlier. "But I can see the extra step I just took was unnecessary. You should be more cautious, sweetheart. Up you go." Grasping her waist, he lifted her onto the seat, her hands gripping his shoulders to keep her balance, his warm breath now fanning her face.

"You just said I was safe with you," she whispered, wishing he would use that tempting mouth to shut her up.

Instead, he tightened his hands and exasperation colored his tone as he drawled, "Turn around and give me your address."

Leslie settled on the wide leather seat, leaned her head back and closed her eyes against her blurred vision, rattling off her address on a sigh.

RESPONSIBILITY. That word had been drilled into Kurt Wilcox's head his entire life. It was why he found himself moving back to Montana after an eight-year absence and why an inebriated woman he didn't know, sporting a bruised cheek was sitting in his truck. He didn't like seeing her face swollen from a would-be mugger's hit any more than he could sit back and do nothing when he'd spotted her leaving the bar in an obvious effort to hide her looped condition. At least taking the time to perform this good deed offered one benefit; it delayed his return to the family ranch and the father he was not looking forward to sparring with again. Eight years wasn't long enough to put aside the hurtful accusations he'd finally tired of hearing and had walked away from.

Kurt slid his gaze toward the attractive blonde, glad her eyes were closed, hiding the shadows of desperation in their blue depths. What self-respecting Master wasn't a sucker for a woman in distress and didn't want to see to her emotional and physical needs? Just because she tugged on his dominant urges didn't mean she would welcome his control or anything else though. Besides, he was seeing her safely home, not planning to stay for a one-night-stand, something he hadn't indulged in since college.

Pulling into the apartment complex just a few blocks from the bar, he cut the engine and nudged her shoulder, eager now to be on his way. No sense in adding complications to his return. There were already enough to overcome as it stood. "Wake up and tell me which apartment is yours."

She moaned, the throaty purr going straight to his cock as she stretched and arched her back. The soft blue dress cinched around the waist with a narrow belt pulled over the soft, round shape of her breasts, her nipples peaking as he watched. He whipped his eyes up to her face to see hers opening wide, the indefinable need reflected in the blue depths almost painful to see.

"Your apartment number," he reminded her in a gruff tone.

She looked around as if confused before nodding and pointing out the window. "That one, third from the end."

"I'll see you to your door." Kurt came around to the passenger side and lifted her down, stepping back before she could lean against him. Gripping her elbow, he gritted his teeth when she weaved alongside him as they strode up the sidewalk. He'd taken the time to stop at the bar to delay his long overdue return, but if the hour grew much later, that delay would extend until morning and give the old man one more thing to take him to task for.

But when she opened the door and then hesitated before entering to look up at him with a desolate expression, Kurt refused to leave until he ensured she would be all right, his father's expectations be damned.

"Will… will you come in? Please?"

8

The whispered plea tugged on his conscience even as he was tempted to lecture her about inviting strangers into her home. "Not a good idea, sweetheart, but yes, I will, just long enough to help you put something on your cheek."

"I know, but sometimes doing the right thing isn't always the best thing either."

She turned her face away before he could gauge her meaning. Pressing a hand to her lower back, he nudged her inside, asking, "Are you in some kind of trouble?"

Flipping on a light switch, she shook her head, tossing her purse toward a chair where it bounced and fell to the floor. "No." She kicked off her shoes and then stubbed her toe against an end table next to a small sofa. "*Ow*, shit!"

"Sit down before you bruise yourself again." Grasping her shoulders, he pushed her onto the sofa with a scowl. "What's your name?"

"Why?" The belligerence behind the suspicion etched on her face amused him.

"I have a newsflash for you. You won't be any safer now that I'm here by withholding your first name." Kurt saw the moment the lightbulb went off in her head.

"I guess you're right. It's Leslie." She tried to smile and winced, reaching up to cradle her hand against her puffy cheek.

"I'm Kurt. Do you have an ice pack in the freezer?" He pivoted and took the four steps to the small refrigerator, noticing the sparseness of her living area extended into the compact kitchen.

"No, at least, I don't think so."

Leslie's cute frown tickled him. As far as drunks go, she was pretty easy to tolerate and talk to. "Never mind, this bag of frozen peas will work just as good." Returning to the sofa, he sat next to her and held the cold vegetable bag against the darkening bruise forming on her face. She flinched but still leaned into him, her eyes conveying an open invitation he was having trouble ignoring the longer he stayed.

"You... you could, maybe take away the... the pain another way." She pressed one pale hand against his denim-covered cock with a deep inhale, dropping her eyes to his lap.

Kurt clenched his jaw and gripped her delicate wrist, determined not to take advantage of her inebriated state. "You would be sorry come morning and a clearer head." He tried to remove her hand, but she was stronger than her slender frame indicated. Not wanting to use force, he left her hand there for now and prayed for restraint.

"But not tonight, and that's all I care about right now." She squeezed his erection and whispered that damnable word again, this time with an aching catch in her voice that shredded his good intentions. "*Please.*"

LESLIE BLAMED the lucky members of The Barn and their recent commitments to their Doms for her uncharacteristic behavior and the lonely desperation plaguing her tonight. This man, Kurt, a virtual stranger, reminded her of those Masters she had trusted with her body, if not her secrets. His large body crowded her on the sofa, his intent looks, take charge manner and gentle hands stirred her arousal, making her pussy throb for more than her vibrator. With her head still in the fuzzy zone, the only coherent thought coming through clear enough to fully comprehend was the quiet emptiness of her apartment that was indicative of all that was missing in her life. If he left, she would have to face that reality yet again, and why do that tonight when tomorrow would come soon enough?

The thick bulge under her hand drew a ripple of longing, an ache for forgetfulness for a short time. The frozen peas had numbed her cheek and she dropped the bag to reach behind his neck and try to pull his head down to meet her lips.

"Son-of-a-bitch, girl, your hand is like ice." Kurt gripped her wrist and tugged her hand down and the other one away from his groin.

Shackling both wrists in one large hand, he held her hands down between them. Leslie's heart pounded and her mouth went dry. This is where any sane woman would become alarmed, but she'd lost her sanity three and a half years ago when she testified against two spoiled, drugged-up teens and their father's threats ended her life as she'd known it. For her, that controlling hold meant she didn't have to think, didn't have to make decisions or worry about doing or saying the wrong thing.

"What's my name?"

A test of her cognizance, but an easy one. "Kurt. Now will you stay?" The tension in her shoulders eased as he nodded, and she didn't let the reluctance on his face bother her.

"Yes, against my better judgment. I hope to God you don't make me regret this tomorrow."

This time it was he who cupped her nape, only she didn't resist as he pulled her up and covered her mouth with his. With his other hand still holding her wrists as he tightened his hold on her neck, she was left with no choice but to open for his slow exploration and to revel in his mastery. A deep-throated moan slipped from her mouth into his as he stroked her tongue, teeth and gums, his lips moving on hers in a constant, sensuous glide. By the time he eased back, they were both breathing heavy and his eyes had softened with a warmth that curled her bare toes.

"You could tempt a saint with that mouth, sweetheart, and I'm no saint." In a smooth move, Kurt brought her hands above her head as he pushed her back onto the couch.

Leslie's breath stalled as he unbuttoned the row of tiny buttons that ran from the scooped neckline to her waist, his eyes on her face as he spread the fabric open and flicked the front catch of her bra.

"Do you still want this?" he asked, cupping one breast and rubbing his thumb back and forth across the nipple.

"Yes, yes, *yes*!" Leslie arched up into his hand, heat spiraling down to her pussy as he plucked at the distended bud with tight pinches. And then he snagged her breath by sending his hat sailing to the floor and dipping his inky black head to her breast.

At the first touch of his lips wrapping around her nipple, she bucked under him; the first strong suction and she mewled, a pitiful sound of need.

"Like that, do you?" he murmured above the throbbing tip before rasping over it with his tongue.

Biting her lip, Leslie watched him shift to her other straining breast then slammed her eyes shut against the searing pleasure of his hot mouth. Thank God he didn't demand an answer. She doubted she could form a coherent thought as he lavished much-needed attention on her nipples, moving back and forth to suckle, nip and lick until he'd turned both peaks into reddened, up-thrust, pulsing aches.

Breathing heavy, she gazed at his flushed, rugged face as he inched downward, those obsidian eyes on her as he once again asked, "Do you still want to continue?"

She clenched her hands in his grip and narrowed her eyes. "If you stop now, I can't be responsible for what I might do." And that wasn't an idle threat. Whether it was this man she craved with such fiery intensity or her self-imposed celibacy that was responsible for her heightened arousal, she didn't know, or care. All she wanted was the sweet oblivion of release to take her away from reality for a while.

"Good enough." Kurt released her hands, rucked up her dress with one hand while fishing a condom from his pocket with the other.

"Let me," she insisted when he took too long in lowering his zipper over his impressive cock. Wrapping a hand around his hot length, she shuddered at the feel of throbbing veins against her palm and the sight of a few pearly drops seeping from his slit. He was thick and long, and she couldn't wait for the burn of his possession.

"Keep that up and this will be over before I get inside you," he growled as she slowly rolled the latex down his rigid cock and then scraped her nails over his large sac. Shoving her hand aside, he ripped off her panties and settled between her splayed legs, one hand slipping between their bodies.

Leslie cried out with his deep fingered thrust, lifting up against his pumping hand. "*Yes!*"

"I guess I don't have to ask again since you're being quite clear. Deep breath, Leslie."

She inhaled, gripping his arms as he surged inside her, stretching un-used muscles and abrading long-neglected nerve endings in one fell swoop. He pulled back and she shook her head, wrapping her legs around his hips. "No, please, don't… just keep going," she begged.

"You're tight. I don't want to hurt you." Ignoring her plea, he retreated and then worked himself back inside her snug sheath much slower. She dug her nails into his biceps and he swore, grabbed her hands and returned them over her head. "Grip the armrest and don't let go until I say. Got it?"

The dark commanding tone of his rough voice tugged at her nipples, prompted her sheath to gush with anticipation. This was what she craved, someone to take her over, giving her no choice but to comply or end it. The past didn't exist and she didn't have to think about tomorrow. Only now mattered.

"Answer me, Leslie," he insisted with a shallow jab.

She nodded, her head bumping his chin. "Yes, I understand."

"Good enough."

Kurt pulled back and then set up a steady rhythm that robbed her of breath and coherent thought. She arched like a bow under his pistoning hips, her pussy clamping around his steely erection, the spasming muscles too slippery to hold him inside her. Her breathing grew ragged as he went deeper, pounded harder between her gripping thighs. Just as the small contractions heralding an orgasm started, he sat back on his knees, grasped her buttocks and lifted her pelvis for even deeper penetration. His face was as hard as his pummeling invasion, those coal black eyes in constant motion, sliding from her face down to their connected bodies and then back up to her face.

Leslie blushed, something she rarely did anymore after becoming a regular member at the club. In this position, every-thing was right *there*, open and on display for both of them to see. In between his jackhammer thrusts and her face, her perspiration shiny breasts jiggled, the reddened tips puckered into tight, up thrusting pinpoints. His focused attention, not only between her legs where her denuded folds clung to his glistening, pumping cock but also checking on her expressions, made it easy to fanta-size he cared for her, in some way. Her pussy quivered around his cock, and heat blurred her vision as she fisted her hands above her to keep from reaching for him.

Kurt admired her control and saw more evidence of a submissive streak in the way she held back. "Now, Leslie," he ground out, sinking balls deep inside her slick pussy, unable to hold back any longer. Her damp muscles squeezed and massaged his thick girth as she climaxed on a gasp, the friction incredibly hot as she bathed him with her creamy release. Letting go with his own orgasm, he groaned at the hot pleasure sweeping up from his balls to spew into the latex, his head stuck in a euphoric fog for several moments before he came down from the high with slower dips inside her snug, quaking body.

"*Jesus*, girl, you could scorch a man alive." Kurt kissed her soft lips, fast and hard and then lifted off her. The sated pleasure softening her blue eyes changed to the same desolate expression from earlier. She made no move to cover herself as he stood next to the couch, gazing down at the carnal picture she presented with her dress scrunched around her waist, breasts pink from his rough face and her bare labia still swollen and wet. "If you want me to stay, you have to say so."

"I want you to stay," she breathed softly without a second of hesitation.

He was afraid she would say that. Well, he'd already taken several risky chances tonight, why not add another? At least he managed to cover his ass when he flicked his phone to record as he'd fished out the condom. A verbal recording proving she was a willing participant would come in handy if tomorrow she woke with lying regrets.

Bending down, those vivid eyes widened in surprise as he lifted her over his shoulder. Her very attractive ass perched so close to his face was too tempting to resist. Swatting one round globe, Kurt turned toward the darkened hall. "Let's take this party to your bedroom then."

Chapter 2

K urt awoke just as the sun was rising, a soft, warm body
wrapped around him. How long had it been since
he'd spent the entire night in a woman's bed? Too
damn long, he mused as he found himself reluctant to disen-
tangle his limbs from Leslie's. Too bad that pesky word, responsibilities, intruded with the break of dawn. She didn't stir as he slid
out of her bed, which was good. Mornings after could be a bitch,
more so if you didn't even know the person's last name, or
anything else about her.

Grabbing his clothes off the floor, he saw more of her room
in the gray light shining through the shades of the one window
than he had last night. Just like in the kitchen and living area of
the small apartment, the lack of personal items, such as knickknacks and pictures, was noticeable. He'd never known any
woman who didn't enjoy displaying collectibles, photos or
sprucing up their place with other decorative items that revealed
facets of their personality, of who they were.

He took one more look at Leslie lying on her stomach, one
hand curled by her face on the pillow, the plump softness of one

smooshed breast visible above the sheet covering her from the waist down. He wondered what heartache she'd been trying to forget last night, figuring his odd reluctance to leave stemmed more from lingering curiosity than anything else. They'd fucked twice more after coming to her bedroom, and she'd embraced his every command with a cock-hardening lack of hesitation. She'd said little except 'please', and that one word whispered with that slight catch in her voice had gotten to him every time.

The carpeted floor muffled his footsteps as Kurt left the room to dress and leave. Making sure the door was locked after stepping out, he strode to his truck. He hoped the stable where he'd left Atlas, his American Quarter horse, was open this early. By the time he hitched the trailer, grabbed a quick breakfast and made the thirty-minute drive to the Wilcox Ranch, it would be mid-morning. Maybe he should have called the house last night and let someone know he wouldn't arrive until today, then again, if his father hadn't driven him away with his accusations eight years ago, he never would have left.

Ninety minutes later, Kurt spotted the ten-foot high iron gates to his family's two-hundred-thousand-acre ranch looming ahead and a heart-wrenching spasm robbed him of breath. Eight years was a long time to deprive himself of the home he loved. He'd been content, if not ecstatic with the life he'd made for himself managing their oil interests in Texas. But the Lone Star State wasn't Montana and living in a Houston high-rise apartment in the country's fourth largest city was a far cry from growing up in the least populated state on acreage that sprawled as far as the eye could see. After the last blow-up with his father, he'd had enough and caved to the bitter regret and anger that had defined their relationship for far too long and moved away. Even now, as he pulled his truck over and soaked up the view of miles and miles of open prairie interrupted in the distance by isolated island ranges he'd longed to set eyes on every morning again, the resentment his father's accusations conjured up still burned a hole in his gut.

God, he'd missed spending his days on this land, his nights in his family home. Not the constant, belittling and guilt-inducing words hurled by his father, but the wide-open spaces dotted with the best prime cattle in the industry all blanketed by a cloudless, clear blue sky; of riding the herd for hours or seeing to the Thoroughbreds; of joking with the hands and falling into bed every night exhausted from the physical activity and a day outdoors. Making the annual, obligatory trip back for the holi-days every year had done little to soothe the ache of separating himself from his home. Sitting in an office all day with a view of downtown Houston just couldn't compare, even if he had enjoyed the new challenge managing their oil interests offered him.

Despite employing over fifty ranch hands, from where Kurt sat, the land appeared isolated. If he looked hard enough, he could spot a few cowpokes among the herds or glimpse one of their prized horses galloping across the wildflower-strewn pasture.

An impatient thump resounded from the horse trailer, Atlas' way of letting him know the stallion was ready to get out of there. Kurt's mouth curled in a humorless grin. Leland Wilcox wouldn't welcome the quarter horse in the stable allotted for his valuable equines, but that was too damn bad. He refused to leave his beloved steed behind and wanted him housed in one of the roomier stalls.

Another kick against the metal back end of the trailer was accompanied by a high-pitched neigh of irritation. "Okay, big guy, I get it." Shifting the gear back into drive, he pulled forward and turned toward the slowly opening gates, waving to employees who noted his arrival. As one of the wealthiest landowners in the state, his father had never spared any expense to protect what had come down to him from his father, and his grandfather before that. Too bad Leland's money couldn't protect his daughter from herself or his wife from cancer.

May as well not go down that road until I have to. He was sure Leland wouldn't let a simple thing like a stroke keep him from reminding Kurt it had been his responsibility to keep his sister, Brittany from self-destructing. When he'd gotten the call three months ago from their manager, Roy Jacobs, informing him of Leland's stroke, he'd flown to Billings and stayed a week round the clock at St. Vincent's Healthcare, ensuring his father was getting the best care despite his usual surly attitude. Before returning to Houston, he'd gotten Leland to promise to give rehab his best shot and offered to run the ranch while he was recovering. He'd always known where his responsibility lay, even if he'd turned his back on it these past years. Coming back home wasn't the hardship though. Dealing with Leland would be.

It took five minutes to drive from the gates to the sprawling Spanish style ranch house he'd grown up in. Pulling in front, he got out and inhaled a deep breath of the fresh, early morning air, catching a whiff of livestock mingling with the sweeter scents of wheat and hay from the fields. They would harvest the summer crops soon, if they hadn't already begun. He wasn't surprised to hear the front door open or Babs' excited squeal of welcome as she came rushing down the porch steps to throw her soft, round arms around him.

Laughing, Kurt hugged her back. "Missed me, did you?"

Leaning back, the older woman gazed at him fondly even as she smacked his arm. "Darn right. I hear you're back to stay. Please tell me that's true."

Roy's wife and their housekeeper for the past thirty years, Babs was the employee he'd missed seeing every day the most. The couple lived in one of the cabins they provided for a few employees and had raised their two children on the ranch, both of whom now lived in the smaller, nearby town of Willow Springs with their own families.

"That's true. Someone has to take over for the old man." He grew serious as he looked toward the house. "Has he been difficult?"

"No more than usual, less than I thought he would be when he returned from the hospital. He's actually been on pretty good behavior ever since you told him you were coming in this week. Although," she scolded, "we were expecting you yesterday."

"Yeah, sorry for the delay. Something came up." More like someone, he mused, thinking of Leslie, and how tempting she looked in her bed as he'd left. At least he'd had the chance to see her blue eyes glaze with passion and then glow with stunned pleasure before leaving. Now he wouldn't have that haunted gaze shadowing their pretty color plaguing his conscience. "Let me get Atlas turned out to pasture and I'll be in. Tell him I'm here, would you?"

"Oh, he already knows. He's been watching out the window. Dr. Hoffstetter will be here at eleven and Mr. Wilcox wanted you here by then."

"That's Willow Springs new physician? He makes house calls?" Kurt cast Babs a skeptical look. "Is Dad sure this guy is on the up and up?"

"See, you do care." Babs' eyes turned watery before she blinked the moisture away. "Yes, he comes with some impressive credentials, including five years as the lead trauma surgeon at Denver Health. He and your father have a love/hate relationship." Her lips quirked, as if she knew what he would say to that.

"Like Leland has with everyone, including me."

She chuckled and gave his arm a slight push. "Go, take care of your horse and I'll tell him you'll be in shortly."

Kurt drove around to the stables where they housed the Thoroughbreds and ushered Atlas out of the trailer. With a coat color somewhere between white and tan and white tail and mane, the stallion was a striking animal and one he'd grown fond of since buying him six years ago. Spending time riding Atlas every day instead of having to settle for weekends at the boarding stables was one of the perks of returning to the ranch he was looking forward to most.

"Here you go, boy." Opening the gate into the pasture behind the stable, he unhooked the lead from his halter and slapped his rump. Atlas took off at an exuberant gallop and it was a pleasure watching his enthusiastic acceptance of his new surroundings. He found a small group of other horses and after a few nips and head butts to establish territory, everyone seemed to get along. With a sigh of inevitability, Kurt turned toward the house and strode across the lawn to check in with his parent before unpacking.

He could hear Leland's brittle tone as he veered toward the master bedroom suite on the south side of the house. Reaching the double doors to his parent's room, he pushed one open and saw him sitting in a wheelchair facing the wide window where he must have watched him walking from the stable. Kurt cut a quick glance toward Cory, his father's private aide, who gave him a welcoming smile.

"Sir, it's good to see you again. Mr. Wilcox is happy you've come back to stay."

Shaking his hand, Kurt glanced at Leland with a lifted brow. "Is that so? Nice to see you again, too, Cory. Dad, have you been giving him a hard time?"

Leland grunted. "Boy's always pestering me to do more. Man can't even get any peace in his own damn room. You're late."

"So I am," he returned without an explanation. Leland's frail appearance jolted Kurt, kept him rooted in place for a moment as he took in the lost weight and the lack of muscle tone in his right arm and leg. So much for hoping for more progress by this time. "Babs said the doctor will be here soon. Anything you want to tell me before he gets his say." Nodding to Cory, he waited until the younger man slipped out before padding over to the man who, for the first time, looked all of his seventy-two years. His mother had been ten years younger than Leland, and yet, had still died in her mid-forties of a cancer all their money couldn't buy off.

"He's okay, he lectures but knows when to quit, unlike Cory." Leland scowled, irritation flashing in his eyes. "That young therapist is a thorn in my side. You know her, she married one of the Dunbar boys."

"I heard last year, Connor and Cade held a double wedding. I was sorry I couldn't make it." As much as he'd wanted to attend his friends' wedding, he couldn't get away from Houston in July. Having spent two weeks here the Christmas before, he'd had a chance to meet Sydney, Cade's wife, and he remembered Tamara from years ago as a cute kid who had eyes only for her neighbor, Connor. The Dunbars lucked out with those girls, both of whom proved to enjoy their dominant control as much as spending time at their private club, The Barn.

Leland snorted again. "About as sorry as you are for taking off in the first place. Your choice."

Kurt couldn't keep from flicking a glance at the ten-by-ten picture of Brittany sitting on the small bedside table with some of her collectible knickknacks surrounding it. His tone carried an edge of warning as he returned his gaze to his father and said, "I'm not going down that road again. You're dealing with a lot, I get that, Dad, and I'm willing to do all I can to ease your burden in running the ranch and help you recover, but I will not rehash Brittany's death or let you continue blaming me. Understood?" He'd decided to pull off the gloves first thing regarding his father's health and any accusations about the drunken car accident that had taken his twenty-year-old sister's life along with three others.

Leland's face clouded with sorrow, his dark eyes shifting from Kurt to out the window and the small, fenced family plot up on a hill. His grandparents, uncle and aunt, mother and sister were buried there, resting, he hoped, in peace.

"I saw you unloading a quarter horse. Nice looking animal."

Kurt shook his head, as if he hadn't heard him right. "Not the response I was expecting. What gives?"

"People change, Kurt, and sometimes life throws you a curve ball that knocks you in the head and wakes you up to a few things." He waved his hand without looking at him. "Go, get settled back in. We'll talk again when the doc gets here."

Reaching out to him for the first time, he squeezed Leland's unaffected shoulder, the muscle bulk a small relief. At least he wasn't letting his good side deteriorate along with the weak side. "Give me an hour." He turned to go, but swiveled his head to say, "His name is Atlas. Maybe, when you're ready, we can go for a ride. I've heard that can be good therapy."

"Don't push it, boy," he growled and Kurt felt better at the return of his disagreeable attitude. It had been so long since he'd seen his accommodating side, he didn't know how to handle it.

As he started hauling his things in from the truck, Kurt listened to Babs bustling in the kitchen and smelled something good as he veered down the hall opposite the one leading to his father's quarters. Four rooms, each with a private bath, were in the east wing of the six thousand square foot house, his room since birth the first one on the right. His sister's across the hall remained closed and he knew, if he were to peek inside, it would look the same as it had almost ten years ago when she'd died. That closed door bothered him as much as the shrine arranged on a table next to the fireplace, right below the big screened television in the den. You couldn't watch TV without her eleven by fourteen inch picture surrounded by the ceramic animals she loved to collect filling your peripheral vision. Her smiling face tugged on his conscience, and his heart.

Grief he understood. Hadn't he succumbed to that emotion upon hearing about the accident that had ended four young lives? Following their mother's death three years earlier, Brittany had turned to alcohol and drugs for solace instead of to him or Leland. He'd tried, God knows how hard he'd tried to straighten her out, get her help and counseling, but nothing stuck. Their father was too awash in his own heartbreak to do anything except tell him to watch out for his sister, and then blame him every time she resorted to her wild ways.

Setting his two largest bags on the bed, he refused to rehash the two years he'd tolerated his father's constant blame following Brittany's death. When he'd made the decision to return home to take over the ranch he'd been groomed to run since childhood, as well as take care of Leland, he'd vowed to let the past go. Now, if only his parent would come around, they might salvage something of their relationship that, at one time, had been very good.

By the time Kurt was putting away the last of his clothes, he heard a car door shut from his open window. Looking out, he saw a tall man with salt and pepper hair and matching goatee carrying a black bag and striding up to the porch. Beating Babs to the front door, he smiled at the short, round woman who tried scowling but couldn't quite pull it off.

"I've got it, Babs. I believe it's the doctor."

"I know, that's why I was in such a rush. I may be pushing sixty, but I've got eyes and that Dr. Hoffstetter is as much man candy as you." She wiggled her eyebrows with a smirk.

Shaking his head, he shooed her back, grabbing for the door handle. "Go finish lunch. I'll invite him to stay."

"On it, but don't take long. We're having fajita chicken salad."

Opening the door, Kurt tried not thinking about marinated chicken tossed with black beans and homemade barbeque ranch dressing, one of his favorites. "Dr. Mitchell Hoffstetter." He held out his hand. "Kurt Wilcox, Leland's son."

"I've heard a lot about you." Shaking his hand, the doctor

removed his Stetson as he entered. "And no, I didn't believe half of it."

Kurt liked him already. "Smart man. You can tell me over lunch what you do believe. It's been a while since I've visited Willow Springs, but I know the town must be grateful for another doctor."

They turned together toward the hall leading to Leland's rooms. "It's a nice place, smaller than I'm used to, but the slower pace suits me. Your father is doing well, but could do better."

"That's just one of the reasons I'm back to stay. With luck, I can help there. I may not be his favorite person, but he'll listen just to get me off his back." It still hurt, even after all this time, to think he might never measure up in his father's eyes again.

Mitchell flicked him a scrutinizing look. "I think you underestimate his feelings for you. I saw his face when he got your call saying you were coming home. I made it my business to do a little digging into your family. You two had it rough losing two family members so close together." A spasm of sorrow crossed his face and darkened his eyes before he cleared his expression. "I'm sorry, I know how difficult that must have been."

Kurt caught the fleeting glimpse of sadness; it was a similar look of heartbreak he'd seen reflected on Leslie's face, in her blue eyes. Like her, this man seemed to want to hide his own painful loss, and he gave him the respect of not prying. "It was, and likely still will be since Leland deals with part of his grief by blaming me for my sister's recklessness that led to her death." He figured airing the dirty laundry was best if the doctor planned to stay this diligent in his care for his contrary patient. "I'll work with him the best I can, that's all I can promise." With a short rap, he entered the bedroom. "Dad, Doc's here."

Kurt stood off to the side while Mitchell did a quick vitals check and made notes before asking Leland how much he was getting out of the chair.

"That girl is a ball buster," Leland snapped, but Kurt noticed the softening of his face when he mentioned Tamara, the physical therapist and his friend, Connor's wife. "Always carrying on about gettin' up, gettin' movin'."

"That's the only way you'll get your strength back, what's possible anyway. You keep sitting around on your butt, you can forget ever sitting on a horse again," Mitchell told him with a bluntness Kurt approved of. Better than anyone else, he knew that was the best way to handle his dad and it appeared it hadn't taken the doc long to learn that.

"If you'd spend less time giving everyone a hard time and put that effort into your therapy, I can clear you for more activity outside the house that much sooner. The choice is yours." Mitchell softened the lecture by patting Leland's shoulder as he pushed to his feet. "Can I tell Mrs. Dunbar to step it up a notch this week?"

Leland cut a quick glance toward Kurt before replying, "Sure. Now that I can rely on my boy to handle things, I can concentrate on myself."

"If you're trying to shame me for staying away, you should know by now it won't work," Kurt retorted. "But the reason for that will remain tabled. I have a lot to do, as you just pointed out." Pivoting, he left as Cory returned for the doctor's instructions.

Veering into the kitchen, he asked Babs, "I'm sorry. I should have asked if you had enough to include the doctor for lunch."

"Already planned on him, so yes."

She waved her hand toward the two place settings on a round, six seat kitchen table under a bay window that offered a sweeping view of their manicured green backyard bordered by low hedges of Taunting Spreading yews. The evergreen foliage of short, dark green needles offered color when the grass died and tolerated winter burn, making it just one of the markers they could rely on when they were forced to deal with chores during the snow season. It had taken Kurt just one time getting disoriented and turned around when he'd tried to find his way from the farthest barn back to the house during a white-out to never make the mistake of not heeding the safety markers around the ranch again. He'd been all of eight years old and had paid the price for disobeying the foreman's instructions to wait for him before heading back. Later, after he'd spent almost an hour lost, came close to succumbing to hypothermia, got his butt blistered and saw tears in his father's eyes for the first time, he realized how lucky he'd been.

For a bad memory, that poignant moment when he'd seen his father's vulnerability when it came to his love for his family was forever seared in his heart. If only Leland could see past his grief over losing both Angela and Brittany long enough to acknowledge his sister, and her inability to cope with their mother's death, was to blame for the events that led up to that car accident. Kurt was no psychologist but suspected his father's difficult struggle with Angela's death hadn't helped Brittany cope, and then to turn her over to Kurt to handle when she lashed out compounded the volatile tenseness they all lived under.

Babs laid her hand on his shoulder, bringing him back to the present. "He's perked up these past weeks, since hearing you were coming back to stay. It won't be like before, Kurt. I just know it, and he's changed since the stroke, mellowed, believe it or not, since he's had time to reflect on his mistakes."

"Let's hope you're right, because I'm in no mood to return to a constant pissing match with him. I can fulfill my obligations to the ranch from another house, if it comes to that."

"Save that threat for when it'll do the most good," Mitchell said, entering the kitchen. "I've seen a change in him lately, one that gives me hope for a fuller recovery. That smells good, if your offer for lunch is still open."

Kurt nodded. "It is. Have a seat."

"You too." Babs pushed Kurt toward the table when he made to help her dish out the salad.

"I can see she's not a woman to argue with." Mitchell's mouth curled, softening his rugged features as he slid into a chair.

"No, definitely not if you want to get fed. Dad's checkup pass the muster?"

"It did." The doctor nodded his thanks as Babs set a large bowl in front of each of them, along with chips and salsa. "I'll take Mr. Wilcox and Cory theirs then head home for a few hours. See you at dinner."

"Thanks, Babs." Kurt sent her a grateful smile, knowing she was giving him a private moment with the doctor and time to settle back in. They discussed Leland's health, a game plan for therapy and prognosis as they ate, the doctor's detailed suggestions and schedule affording Kurt hope his dad would enjoy another ten healthy, if not as robust years.

"That all sounds good," he commented, refilling their iced tea glasses. "I'll see he keeps to the schedule and start bringing him in for checkups, and therapy if needed. We can't expect Tamara to keep coming out here."

Mitchell hesitated before asking with seeming nonchalance, "Do you know her and her husband well?"

"The Dunbars? Yes, Caden a little better than Connor as he and I went through high school together. I hung out with both of them some, along with Grayson Monroe before I moved to Houston. Why do you ask?"

Shoving back, Mitchell crossed one ankle over his opposite knee and pinned Kurt with a direct look. "If you know them that well, I'll assume you've heard about a private club they own."

"The Barn." Kurt cocked his head, sizing Mitchell up, reading between the lines. "Are you interested as an experienced Dom or for checking out the lifestyle?"

"So, I guessed right. You're a member?"

"Not officially. They opened the place a few years after I left. I've attended as a guest numerous times since then, whenever I've made the trip back, but never joined. I planned to discuss it with Caden this week. We're getting together at the diner for dinner on Thursday. Care to join us?"

He huffed a rueful laugh. "That was easy enough. Thank you, yes. And to answer your previous question, I've been a player since my twenties, married my third sub and we were members of a club in Denver for ten years."

Kurt frowned, glanced at his bare ring finger and lifted an inquiring brow. "Divorced?"

"Widowed," he returned curtly. "Two years now. I just turned forty-two, she died of ovarian cancer. No kids." He shrugged. "I figured I'd save you from either asking or speculating. I also figure you have an inkling of how difficult it's been, given your own losses."

"I'm sorry, and yes, I do. A spouse, though, is a different, more intimate relationship than a sister or parent. Especially, I imagine, when you are lucky enough to enjoy a Dom/sub life-style together." Unbidden, Leslie's face popped into his head, her features etched with emotional pain, and he wondered if she had lost someone, or had anyone else to fill the void. Maybe not, since she had chosen to ease her pain and loneliness with a one-night stand with him. Since it would be a waste of time mulling over questions about last night, he shoved aside those thoughts. She'd intrigued him, had drawn on his protective instincts as much as his dominant cravings more than anyone else, but the odds of seeing her again were minimal, at best.

"No experience in commitment yourself?" Mitchell inquired.

"Not yet, and at forty, it's not likely to happen. Although, the Dunbars' marriages just last year came unexpectedly, so anything's possible." Rising, they rinsed their dishes and Kurt walked him out, saying, "I'll meet you at the diner, say six-thirty. Does that work for you?"

"It does, thanks." Mitchell jerked his head toward the house as he opened the truck door. "Good luck with your old man."

"I'm going to need it."

HOW COULD I have been so stupid? Leslie lost count of how many times she asked herself that question by the time she sat down to dinner Saturday evening. Due to her hangover, food hadn't appealed to her all day until now. If she could just quit rehashing her idiocy of the night before, she would enjoy the plate of shrimp linguini sitting before her.

With a sigh, she twirled the pasta on her fork and admitted for the hundredth time she should never had let her melancholy mood get the better of her, for all the good that did. As if relocating from Reno, the only place she'd ever lived, to Billings, Montana hadn't been enough to adjust to three and a half years ago, giving up all contact with her sister and friends had turned out to be an even bigger sacrifice than she'd imagined. Her sister's tear-filled, devastated voice when Leslie broke down and explained how a threat from the defendant's rich father following her damning testimony jeopardized her safety would be forever etched in her mind. Despite the eight-year gap in their ages and the fact Roslyn lived in Canada and she didn't get to see her much, she missed talking to her and her sons desperately.

Even though they'd only allowed her to tell her immediate family goodbye, there was no doubt her friends and coworkers had read about the murder and the eyewitness testimony against the eighteen- and nineteen-year-old sons of one of Reno's wealthiest, well-known families that had put the young men behind bars. The cops and prosecutors had tried to get a judge to allow her to tape her testimony, but money and influence spoke louder than their arguments. Her name was kept out of the papers, but two and two was still easy to add up and she didn't doubt her friends had connected her sudden disappearance with the recent prominent court case.

Leslie took a bite of the buttery pasta, casting a furtive glance toward the time displayed on her cell phone sitting next to her plate. There was still plenty of time to eat, dress and make the thirty-minute drive to the secluded club situated between Billings and the small town of Willow Springs. Her one-night stand with a stranger had scratched just the surface of the lonely itch that still plagued her with despondency today. His focused attention that had driven her to orgasm several times had only whetted her appetite for more and reminded her of all she was missing out on by staying away from The Barn.

Recalling the look in Kurt's black eyes as he'd gazed at her, his heavy body thrusting inside her with deep, womb-touching plunges while whispering commands in her ear she was helpless to resist brought on a familiar surge of heat neither her hand nor vibrator were enough to defuse. Between his chivalry in coming to her aid, insistence on seeing her safely home and sexual, take charge control, he'd given her all she'd ached for. Too bad waking up to face another day alone brought back the cold reality of her current life – a life that held no future or allowed for anything more than those come-and-go encounters with both men and friends.

No, she thought, forcing herself to take another bite, she wasn't ready to return to The Barn tonight, not until she was convinced she could do so without resenting the people she'd met and liked so well. It wasn't their fault she would never have what they were lucky enough to find. Following the second week of her absence at the club, Sydney's call of concern had given Leslie a much-needed boost of pleasure. When Nan phoned a few days later and filled her in on her successful trip back to New Orleans to testify against the man who had kidnapped and abused her, the temptation to accept her friend's invitation to a girls' night out celebration had come close to crumbling Leslie's resolve to keep her distance for a while. Considering the way she'd held herself back from getting too close to anyone, their overtures meant a lot and offered a comfort they wouldn't understand.

Leslie resigned herself to spending the evening working on lesson plans for her second graders instead of indulging in another night of hot, sweaty, mindless sex. Someday she would get herself under control again and accept her fate for doing the right thing, at least enough to play without revealing her jealousy or despair over everything she'd lost.

Chapter 3

Kurt drove into the small town of Willow Springs Thursday evening looking forward to reconnecting with his friends. Spending the last few evenings catching up on the business side of ranching, the days getting back into the groove of spending hours in the saddle instead of behind a desk and having pissing contests with his father, left little time for socializing. Thinking of Leland brought a frown to his face as he turned toward the town square. He could handle his cantankerous side, God knows he'd had enough experience. It was the minute glimpses of longing in his eyes Kurt had caught a few times that had thrown him for a loop. The quick way Leland would turn aside drew Kurt's curiosity, but then he'd whip toward him again with some sarcastic snipe, the softening on his face gone.

"Stubborn son-of-a-bitch," he grumbled as he parked in front of Dale's Diner on the corner of Main. The picturesque fountain in the center of the square bubbled with a flow of water that kids loved to play in. The one-hundred-year-old buildings that still housed the city offices, sheriff's precinct and library were a far cry from the modern high-rises of downtown

Houston where he'd worked. Damn, he thought on a deep inhale of fresh air, it was good to get back to his roots, and know he was home to stay this time. Regardless of his tenuous relationship with his father, he vowed to make it work this time around.

"Is it true, you're back for good?" Caden Dunbar demanded to know as soon as he hopped out of his truck and strolled around to greet Kurt.

"If Leland and I don't end up killing each other. Good to see you again." He shook the rancher's hand before turning to his brother. "You too, Connor. I hope you don't mind but I invited Doctor Mitchell Hoffstetter to join us. He was out to see Dad and brought up hearing about the club."

Connor nodded, his blue eyes twinkling as he replied, "We've met. He's a good guy."

Caden snorted as he opened the door to the diner. "You didn't think so when you heard Tamara would be working with the new hot doctor."

With an unconcerned shrug and rueful grin, Connor quipped, "A guy's gotta look after what's his."

"That sure is a change of heart from a short time ago," Kurt drawled, following them inside the diner and getting his first appreciative whiff of as close to home cooking as you could get in a restaurant.

"The same could be said for you, but I for one am damn glad you've come to your senses. There's no excuse for you not to become a full-time member now." Caden smiled at the older woman glaring at them from behind the long counter as a 1950s oldie kicked out from the jukebox. "Hey, Gertie, look who's back."

Gertie answered with her usual bluntness. "I see. You done with the big city yet?"

"Yes, ma'am. At least until my old man kicks me out." Gertie and her husband, Dale had opened the diner eons ago and she

34

continued to run the place with an iron hand and deep caring for the town folk after his death.

"Well, don't just stand there and expect me to escort you to your usual table." She jerked her head toward the far corner booth. "The sheriff and our new doc beat you here."

Chuckling, Kurt tossed his hat on a hook next to several others, winking at her as they crossed the black and white checkered floor. "I've missed you, Gert."

"Don't call me Gert or you can forget the free piece of cherry cobbler I have saved for you," she snapped.

"Slip of the tongue." Still smiling, he slid into one of the chairs facing the long, curved seating against the wall, holding out his hand to Grayson Monroe. "How the hell are you, Monroe?"

Grayson's lips tipped up at one corner, shifting the toothpick he was always chewing on. "Good, and happy to welcome you back. Hopefully, adding two new members will keep the subs from complaining about too many Doms getting hitched."

"Speaking for myself, I don't have a problem filling in the gap." Kurt nodded at the doctor. "Mitchell, meet the Dunbars, the other two owners of The Barn."

It took less than ten minutes of good-natured ribbing and small talk to know Mitchell would fit in as well as Kurt always had. By the time Gertie helped their waitress, Barbara serve their burgers and fries, talk had switched from the club to horses, a passion they discovered, that Mitchell shared with them.

"Buying my own mount is one of my top priorities now that I've settled in and started work," the doctor said after Caden filled Kurt in on the new breeding program he and Connor were undertaking. "Is there a boarding facility nearby? I don't want to stable one as far away as Billings."

"Are you living in town?" Kurt asked before diving into his double cheeseburger with relish.

Mitchell nodded. "Just put a down payment on a place over

on Bluff, but don't think a horse or the good sheriff here would take kindly to me housing it in the back yard."

Grayson's lips quirked, his version of a grin. "So I don't have to cite you, why don't you board with my bay, Thunder? I've got a two-stall stable and a few acres just outside of town."

"Thank you. I'll let you know."

Kurt crunched on a fry as he made an offer of his own. "You're welcome on the ranch, but the distance is twice what Grayson's place is."

"And so is our place, but we've got another offer on the table, if you ever need it," Caden put in. "We're all passionate about our horses, in case you couldn't tell. You're from Denver, right?"

Mitchell nodded, swallowing a bite before answering, "Originally from Maryland, but did my residency in Denver and stayed."

"Some damn fine livestock hail from there. If you're interested in a Thoroughbred, I can give you a good price." Kurt figured that was the least he could do in return for the care he was giving his dad.

"I'll see what you have, but I'm more inclined toward adopting a rescue with issues and working with it. I enjoy a challenge and like to keep busy."

A shadow of grief crossed Mitchell's face again, and Kurt saw his friends noticed it also. None of them would pry, and he wouldn't reveal the little Mitchell had told him. "Those animals are capable of breaking you if you're not careful. Feel free to come to any of us for help, or just advice if you need it."

Connor smiled. "I love the workout of breaking in a new bronc, but for any more of a challenge than that, I'll stick with my newbie sub. She still has a lot to learn."

That is not envy tightening my gut, Kurt insisted. Yeah, he'd had fleeting moments wondering what it would be like to settle down with one woman who knew him as well as he knew her. But, for all the relationships he'd enjoyed, none had left a lasting impression or resulted in strong enough feelings to contemplate making it permanent. There were a few vanilla affairs he remembered with fondness, and a few Dom/sub pairings he recalled with interest in a repeat if they were both ever so inclined, but that was as far as his emotional investment with anyone had gone.

A pretty face surrounded by a swath of dark blonde hair popped into his head again. It must be worry over Leslie's fragile state that kept the memory of their one night together a week ago in the forefront of his mind. If he couldn't forget her within the next week, he might consider driving back to Billings and stopping by her apartment to set his mind at ease. He doubted she would welcome a surprise visit, but that would be too bad if that was what he needed to do to settle his conscience.

"Where'd you go?"

Caden's amused voice pulled Kurt's head out of the clouds. "Sorry, just thinking about something. I need to get back." He pushed away from the table, tossing down a generous tip and picking up his tab. "I'll pay my membership online in the morning and see you tomorrow night at the club. How about you, Mitchell?"

The doctor nodded. "I'll do the same." His gaze swept the Dunbars and Grayson as he said, "Thank you for the invite."

"Welcome aboard. Come early and we can give you a tour of the place," Caden offered as Kurt lifted his hand in farewell and turned to leave.

"It's good to have you back," Gertie commented when she met him at the cash register. "You get your old man out and bring him in. He's stayed to himself way too long. Grief's going to be there whether he sits around moping or not."

"He's lost a spouse and a child, and since I can't relate to either, I don't push," Kurt returned. "But I know you can commiserate with the loss of a spouse."

"The work helps. Your daddy can't get out and work the

ranch now, but he can come into town and shoot the breeze. You tell him I said to quit being so lazy and ornery."

Kurt grinned. "I'll do that, Gertie. Thanks."

Stepping out into the cooler evening air, he looked up at the star-studded inky sky, hoping Leland was settled in bed in front of his television by the time he got home. To his surprise, the few times his dad had brought up Brittany in the past few days, it was without leveling an accusation of blame on Kurt. While he couldn't say Leland's overall attitude had done a one-eighty, he could admit it appeared he was trying to get along. With luck, Kurt would get caught up on the business side of the ranch before his old man showed his true colors and they got into it again.

LESLIE ENTERED her favorite corner market and stepped into a nightmare. As if hearing the cruel mocking laughter echoing from the front wasn't bad enough, the loud rapport of a gunshot as she stepped around the corner sent a wave of terror through her. Shock rooted her in place as she witnessed the two teens putting a bullet in the owner's head, the spray of blood and brain matter sending bile rushing up to clog her throat. Without thinking, she dashed back out before either assailant noticed her, jumped into her car and sped toward the nearest police precinct. Knowing her fond memories of Alessandro, the owner, were forever blocked by that gruesome, heartbreaking, frightening moment blinded her with tears as her whole body shook in reaction. On her way home from a date that had ended like all the others, with little interest in taking things further, a sudden craving for Alessandro's cannoli had hit her as she'd passed by and noticed a light still shone in the back window.

Little did she know that identifying the Glascott brothers as Alessandro's killers would be the beginning of another bad dream.

Leslie rolled over in bed with a groan, wishing the memories away so she could get back to sleep. But as she drifted off again, the cold eyes and sneering faces of those two wealthy, pampered young men intruded once again.

"Are you sure, positively sure, the two defendants are the ones you saw kill Alessandro Carmichael on the night of April sixth?"

Leslie shifted her gaze from the DA to the two unrepentant teens. Only eighteen and nineteen and the young men would spend the rest of their lives behind bars. "Yes, I'm sure. Those two are the ones I saw."

Jason Glascott surged to his feet before his high-priced attorney could stop him. "I'll bury you, bitch!" he roared as he made to climb over the table. While he was quickly restrained, his brother gave her a cold stare and ran one finger across his throat, mimicking a knife slice.

Shivering in reaction as the courtroom erupted in a frenzy of shouting, Leslie grabbed Detective Reynold's arm as soon as he rushed to her side. "Come on. You're done here," he said in a tight voice, shielding her as much as possible as he guided her toward the exit.

Just as they reached the wide double doors, the teens' father, Edwin, brushed by her, close enough to bend down and whisper, "You'll never be safe," before disappearing into the crowd.

Jerking upright in bed, Leslie swiped a shaking hand over her damp brow as she blinked awake. She thought she was over the nightmares that had plagued her for months after she entered the Witness Protection program. The attempted mugging last week must have affected her more strongly than she'd first thought, triggering the fear and uncertainty of her circumstances again.

"Enough already," she muttered, flinging the covers off and sliding out of bed. The early morning sky shone dull and gray through the closed blinds and she could feel her spirits toward facing another weekend alone taking a nosedive. Padding into the bathroom, she stripped off her nightshirt and stepped into the miniscule shower, contemplating returning to The Barn tonight. She needed to force herself out of the funk she'd allowed herself to wallow in for too long, the 'poor me' pity party that had led her to risk a one-night stand with a stranger.

But hot damn, what a stranger, and what a night. Just thinking about

Kurt and the orgasms he had wrung from her with his take charge dominance could still produce small shivers of remembered pleasure. When he'd tossed her on her bed, lifted her legs over his shoulders and buried his mouth between them, she'd splintered apart within seconds, and that was only minutes after climaxing under him on the couch. But the way he'd awoken her several hours later would be forever seared into her memory. To erase the remnants of her bad dreams, she leaned against the tile wall and tried to remember that night.

Leslie groaned in groggy awareness of hard hands rolling her over onto her stomach. Snuggling down into her pillow with intentions of going back to sleep, she was jarred into full wakefulness by a sharp slap on her right buttock. "Oh, God," she mumbled into the pillow when the next cheek bouncing smack landed on her left globe. She refused to look around at the stranger delivering that welcome stinging burn, a desired sensation she hadn't felt in way too long. The dark room lent an intimacy to the shift of their naked bodies against the sheets and their deep breathing. He tapped the under curve of her right buttock and then cupped the fleshy mound in his calloused palm to squeeze the tormented flesh.

"Nice ass," he whispered in her ear, his warm breath drawing goose-bumps along her arms. "Reach above you, Leslie, and hold onto the head rail. Do not let go. Understood?"

"Yes," she whispered with a delicate shiver as she groped above her for a handhold. Wrapping her hands around the metal bar, she tightened her grip, recalling the oddness of voluntary bondage she'd experienced earlier on the couch. She was used to physical restraints ensuring her compliance, making it easy for her to cede to the wishes of whichever Master she was submitting to. She liked tugging against the bondage, got off on knowing she had no choice but to obey or end the scene with one word. This nonrestrictive bondage brought about a whole new wave of self-awareness that gave her something else to think about except the risk of inviting a stranger into her home, and her bed.

"Good girl. You're not new to spanking, are you?"

Kurt punctuated his inquiry with a harder swat that drew a gasp from

Leslie and prompted her into lifting for another. His low chuckle reverberated down her spine as he caressed her butt. "That's a good enough answer." He nipped the tender spot between her neck and shoulder, the prick of pain and his next command curling her toes. "Spread your legs. Wider," he growled when she didn't go far enough.

Cool air brushed over the delicate flesh of her bare labia as she spread her legs the width of the double bed. Keeping up with stretches and a few dance moves from her years of ballet lessons had kept her flexible, which had come in handy when she'd started exploring the BDSM lifestyle as a means of escape from the upheaval of her entire life.

"I like the way you obey without question." He stroked one hand down the inside of her thigh, the scrape of his rough callouses along her soft skin eliciting another groan and twitch of her buttocks.

"I like the way you touch me," she returned in a low voice, the darkness lending her courage to speak her mind, something she'd never done at the club. When there, she preferred remaining a willing but unassuming player so as not to call attention to herself or unintentionally invite an expansion on a Dom/sub relationship or any of her friendships. What would be the point of bonding with others when she knew getting close to her could turn toxic without warning? After the police had deflected two attempts on her life before stripping her of her real identity and everything else she'd ever known, she didn't doubt Edwin Glascott's threat against her, or the risk to others after her dear neighbor was injured when visiting her.

"It appears we're a good match then." She stiffened and he rolled on top of her, pinning her to the mattress with over six feet of rippling muscles, his heavy erection coming to rest between her buttocks as his large sac bounced against her pussy. "Don't worry. I'm well aware this is an irresponsible, one-time fuck. And when I say irresponsible, I'm talking about both of us. Remember, don't let go, say red if you want to end this."

Leslie didn't reply, couldn't answer as he kissed, licked and nipped his way down her back until he reached her butt. Once there, he snagged her breath as he cupped her cheeks, holding them propped up for his devious mouth. The brush of soft lips drew more goosebumps; slow, wet tongue strokes produced heat and dampness inside her quivering pussy; pin-pricking bites of discomfort sent a rush of hot pleasure spiraling through her veins. The chill from losing her cover warmed and her tense muscles grew lax. The attention to her backside was new and exciting, transporting her to an altogether new plane where nothing existed, nothing mattered but the slow-building euphoria spreading outward from her buttocks.

A cry spilled from her throat as Kurt released one cheek, cupped that hand between her legs and pressed hard. "You're so fucking responsive. I like that, too. Wet and soft. What more could I ask for or need?"

"I need more," Leslie rushed to say.

"Mmm, not yet. I'm not done playing." He inched a broad thumb between her cheeks and pressed against the puckered rim of her anus.

She squirmed against the pressure against both areas, and the harder he pressed the more she shifted under him. As she started to close the gap in her legs to aid in holding him there, a stab of vicious pain from a tight pinch lanced one tender fold. "Crap!" She tried to spring up, to get away from the throbbing ache, but he gripped her thigh with a dark warning.

"Give me your safeword or be still. If you release your hands, I'll walk out now."

She shook, inhaled and slowly repositioned her legs outward. "No, I don't want to safeword out. Please. You just took me by surprise. No one's ever…"

"Good. I like knowing I can give you a new experience."

A shudder went through her body as he worked two fingers inside her pussy, stretching unused muscles and stroking over neglected nerve endings until Leslie spasmed with a gush of responsive cream.

"Nice." Kurt shifted up to whisper in her ear. "Now, let's work together to make it even nicer."

His voice seeped inside Leslie, the dark room enhancing the deep rumble. Then he leaned back, grabbed her hips, pulled her to her knees and grasped her right hand off the rail above her. He didn't give her time to think about the odd position of holding one arm above her in a tight grip with her face and chest flat and hips levered as he drew her hand down between her legs, his next command heating her blood to the boiling point.

"*Use one finger on your clit while I continue exploring. You have a nice tight pussy, and I want to feel you squeezing my cock again in a minute.*"

Twisting her head, Leslie could barely make out his shape kneeling behind her as he guided her middle finger between her folds along with his. "This is…" Embarrassing. Exciting. Disturbing. Arousing. She rasped her swollen clit, the brush of his finger alongside hers conjuring up all of those emotions. He thrust and stroked as she twirled around the bundle of sensitive tissues.

"This is what? New?" Kurt brushed over her clit with her. "Exciting? Because it is for me. Keep going."

She bit her lip as he pulled out of her just when her sheath convulsed in small spasms, the clutches heralding a climax his withdrawal put on hold. Groaning in frustration, she plucked at her clit, struggling to hold back until he joined her again.

"Good girl." Gripping her wrist, he pulled her hand back and pushed through her slick folds to take its place. She sighed as he stretched and filled her with one deep thrust then gasped as he instructed, "Press your clit against my cock as I fuck you. Like this." Wrapping one hand around her hip, he held her still, rooted out her clit and pressed it against his thick erection as he pumped inside her. "Now, you take over."

Leslie thought there wasn't anything she hadn't seen or tried in the three years she'd enjoyed exploring alternative sex, but she'd thought wrong. Sparks shot from her nub straight up her core as he pummeled her depths with deeper, harder plunges, the tight press of those sensitive tissues against his rigid hardness unlike anything she'd experienced before. The warmth of his flesh seeped through the condom, his steely length almost painful as he rasped back and forth, abrading her clit. Tremors erupted deep inside her as his cock jerked, the onset of her orgasm bathing his shaft with a slick gush. Her muscles squeezed in uncontrollable spasms as she rode out the pleasure with as much force as he rammed into her with his own climax.

Their heavy breathing resonated in the room, her soft cries mingling with his guttural grunts and low curses. Leslie basked in the mindless ecstasy, the rough possession and the temporary escape she'd needed from her loneliness.

The water started to cool, pulling Leslie out of her daydream of that night. Maybe returning to the club tonight was what she needed to put Kurt and her only one-night stand behind her. Would spending a few hours seeking another temporary relief from her loneliness be worth the face-to-face reminders of what she would never have? She honestly didn't begrudge her friends' newfound happiness, and she had to move on some time, needed to come to terms with her fate regardless of the pain. Unless Edwin Glascott and his sons either all keeled over or had a change of heart concerning her part in putting Jason and Jake behind bars for the next forty years, she was stuck living without a commitment to either friendships or a relationship.

Cursing the family who thought their wealth meant they could do as they pleased without consequences, she decided the only way to put one unforgettable night behind her was to replace it with something just as intense, just as pleasurable.

By the time Leslie turned off the highway onto the narrow, tree-lined dirt road that led to the club later that night, those pesky doubts were starting to intrude again. For almost three years she'd looked forward to the weekends and the hours she would spend at the converted barn. But as she reached the gravel parking area in front of the two-story structure nestled in a wide copse, she spotted the Dunbars walking in together. Parking behind two rows of other vehicles, she watched Cade sling an arm around Sydney and pull her close as he opened one of the double-wide doors. Even from several feet away, sitting in the dimly lit lot, Leslie could make out the redhead's smile. Connor and Tamara followed them, Connor's laugh sifting through her open window. The swat he delivered on his wife's butt must have been in playful retaliation for whatever she'd said since it drew a giggle from Tamara instead of a painful gasp.

No matter how often she played with a Dom, or how much pleasure she reaped from a scene, she would never enjoy the fruits of a close bond, one that made such moments so spontaneous and fun. As she changed her mind and pulled back out,

Leslie vowed to come to terms with her life as it was now. With her thirty-fifth birthday coming up in November, the time for wishing she could change the past was long over. There must be a way to reconcile with her fate without being so petty as to stay away from people she'd come to like just because their circumstances had changed for the better. She would work hard at finding it and then come back, when she was sure she could do so without envying others.

NAN SLID out of Dan's truck and turned to watch the small Mazda exit the parking lot. Frowning, she glanced from the taillights to her fiancé. "Wasn't that Leslie?"

"I don't know, I didn't get a good look. Why?" Clasping her elbow, he steered her toward the doors.

"I'm pretty sure it was." Puzzlement and worry tightened her muscles. "She hasn't shown up here for several weeks, and now she's leaving without coming in. I wonder what's going on with her."

Dan's lips quirked as he gazed down at her with warm dark brown eyes. No matter how he looked at her, she never failed to respond with a rush of pleasure. After all the Doms she'd enjoyed playing with the past five years, he was the only one who still did it for her in every way, on every level.

"I'm sure if she wants to confide in anyone here, she will."

"Maybe. She's always kept from getting too close to anyone, too involved with any of us girls, or you Doms. It might be time for a shopping trip to Billings." Entering the club's playroom from the foyer, a familiar thrill shot through her as the sounds and scenes of the kinks she got off on resonated around the cavernous space. Nodding toward a table close to the bar in the center of the lower level, she said, "There's Sydney and Tamara. Do you mind if I join them for a few minutes, Sir?" Falling into submissive mode here at The Barn always came easily despite her natural, independent nature when away from the sex-charged atmosphere.

"Go ahead." Dan nudged her forward with a hand on her butt. "Meet me at the bar in fifteen minutes."

As Nan watched him stroll across the room, his tall, broad shouldered, slim-hipped frame and tight buttocks showcased in snug denim made her itch to call him back and get started on scratching. But first, she intended to enlist help tracking down Leslie, and her reason for staying away. It wasn't that long ago she'd learned the hard way that keeping her distance from those who cared about her wasn't the best way to work through a difficult time. She and Leslie weren't close, not like she was with her best friend, Tamara, and now Sydney and Avery. But she still didn't want her to make the same mistake Nan had months ago.

"Oh, we have got to go shopping again. I want something like that." Sydney eyed Nan's latex, thigh-high stockings that showcased her long legs below her matching leather thong and corset set with envy.

Sliding into a chair, Nan crossed her legs with a smirk. "Caden would swallow his tongue. I'll show you where you can get something similar. In fact, that'll fall right in with what I want to run by you two, and Avery when she gets here. I think I just saw Leslie leaving. Did she even come in?"

Tamara shook her head. "She wasn't inside when we got here about ten minutes ago. It's still early and no one has ventured upstairs yet, so we likely would have seen her. I wonder what's going on with her." Concern clouded her gray eyes.

"Yeah, me too. So, intervention time?" Nan asked both of them.

Sydney shrugged and sent a sly glance toward Tamara. "Why not? We butted in with Tam. May as well nag Leslie about whatever has kept her away."

Nan flipped Tamara a grin and then said, "I can do

Wednesday since I close early. I know she teaches, so we can shop first then pick up something to eat and show up at her place. One of you will have to get her address from the club's membership form."

"No warning ahead of time? I like that but she may not," Sydney warned. "You've known her the longest, Nan."

"And yet I don't know much about her, and we've never socialized outside of here. I'm not sure if she's ever even come into Willow Springs."

"We should have extended an invitation sooner. I only know her well enough to say hi, and now I feel bad about that," Tamara said.

"Don't. She's shied away from getting close for a reason. If she doesn't want that to change, we'll respect her wishes, but it won't hurt to extend an offer of friendship that includes sympathetic ears if she wants to talk. In the meantime, who the hell are those two?" Nan pointed toward two newcomers settling on stools at the bar, both men well over six foot. The one with coal black hair and matching eyes was just as panty-melting as his friend who wore his wavy, salt and pepper hair long enough to tie back like Connor did, his matching goatee framing a sexy mouth.

Tamara feigned a lustful sigh. "That's Master Mitchell on the right with the long hair I'd love to tug out of that leather band. He's the new doctor in town and I get to ogle him at work."

Nan placed her hand over her heart. "I do believe I've put off getting a pap smear for way too long."

Sydney almost spilled her drink on a choked laugh. "You moron. I'm drooling over Master Kurt. Caden said he went to school with him but he moved to Texas years ago. He's just returned to take over running the family spread for his ailing father. According to hubby, the Wilcox family can trace their roots in Montana back decades and they're listed in the top ten of wealthiest families in the state."

Nan raised a slim brow at that information and then spotted

Dan coming toward her. "Uh, oh. I think Master Dan caught me staring." Pushing to her feet, her pulse skipped a beat and her nipples peaked as he frowned at her. "Gotta go. Let's meet at the tea shop around two on Wednesday."

Watching her hightail it over to her fiancé, Tamara giggled. "She's still the only one I know who looks forward to a punishment."

"Oh, I don't know about that. We may not like them as intense as she does, but you can get into a long session over Connor's knees just like I can with Caden," Sydney pointed out.

"Yeah, you're right. And now that you've planted that in my head, it's time to join Connor upstairs. Catch you later."

Chapter 4

Kurt hefted the saddle onto Atlas' back, eager to get started on the day's chores. Damn but it felt good working outdoors again, riding every day and settling in to managing the ranch again. Even dealing with his father's surly attitude the last few mornings hadn't dimmed his enthusiasm for the long hours of physical labor. He understood Leland was dealing with a lot of changes in his life, both physical and mental. It would be difficult for anyone who was used to a physically active life to lose so much ability. What he didn't understand was his obstinance when it came to doing the physical therapy that would help him regain some of that strength back.

"Stubborn old man," he muttered under his breath as he tightened the cinch strap, ensuring his saddle wouldn't slip. The sun already shone bright enough to warm his back and shoulders as he led the stallion out of the stables and waved to the group of hired hands mounting up for fence repairs. Usually by early September, they would start noticing cooler temperatures, but this year it looked like they were in for a few unseasonably warm weeks nobody was complaining about.

"Are you referring to your father?" Roy asked with a grin, overhearing him as he rode up.

"Who else? I left him arguing with Cory about going into Willow Springs for therapy instead of having the therapist come out here. It would do him good to get out." Kurt swung up into the saddle and nudged his hat down to shield his eyes from the bright glare as they rode out side-by-side.

Roy nodded. "I agree. When he's ready, I'll help get him up into a saddle again, go along on a ride if you want. That might be enough incentive to spur him along."

"I've already mentioned it, and he seemed pleased with the idea. But when I brought up changing his therapy sessions to the clinic on Monday, he bit my head off and has refused to discuss Cory driving him in for two days now." As they rode past the family burial plot, he shifted his gaze toward the headstones and fresh flowers adding color to the drab gray slabs.

"The anniversary of Brittany's death is coming up next month. Leland is always at his worst in the fall," Roy reminded him.

"Yeah, I remember." That was one of the reasons Kurt had waited to make his annual trip back home until the end of each year. It didn't surprise him to hear Leland's grief and anger hadn't eased during the years he'd lived in Houston. Any day now, Kurt expected his dad to throw her death in his face, blame him once again for not controlling his sister's behavior. Not once had his father given him credit for getting Brittany into counseling, for cutting off her allowance in the hopes that would curtail her efforts to buy alcohol and drugs, or for sending the cops after her when she'd resorted to stealing from the family safe, which had resulted in mandatory rehab. "Let's ride. I need to clear my mind of what's waiting for me at the end of the day."

Along with riding the fence line looking to repair downed sections, Kurt and the cowpokes mingled with the herds, interacting with the cattle in a calm fashion to keep their stress level down. Like with people, stress could render beef cattle more susceptible to disease. From what he had observed since returning, he estimated close to a thousand head were nearing the ideal weight of between one thousand and twelve hundred pounds and were old enough to take to market and sold for the highest dollar. But the Wilcox family had always juggled several businesses, including horse breeding and oil, not to mention the investments of their capital. All of which fell to him to stay on top of. While he enjoyed managing the business side of his family's wealth, nothing beat spending a few hours riding the wide-open spaces with the view of pine-covered mountains rising up into the clear blue sky, stopping along the way to mend downed fences and check their security system. Not all of their land was fenced in, but at least two-thirds was.

As he hammered a board into place with a breeze tickling the back of his sweaty neck, Kurt's mind wandered to the evening he spent getting to know the members of The Barn, and how his thoughts were constantly disrupted by intruding memories of those few hours he'd enjoyed with Leslie. It was only natural, wasn't it, to wonder, and worry about the woman with the haunted eyes and the desperate pleas? He figured the only way to settle his conscience was to make another trip into Billings with the sole purpose of looking her up and checking on her welfare. He figured once he did that, he could put her out of his mind and get on with entertaining some of the eager submissives he'd met at the club. Besides reconnecting with Caden, his best friend from school, that was one of the perks of returning home, and a great outlet to relieve some of the stress from dealing with his father on a daily basis.

Kurt returned to the house at noon, sweaty, dirty, aching in a good way and ready to put a few hours in at his desk right after lunch. As soon as he stepped inside and heard Leland's belligerent yelling from his room, he knew a shower and food would have to wait.

"I said no, and I meant it! One more word and you're fired."

With a sigh and a surge of muscle-tightening anger, he strode down the hall and flung open the door without knocking. "What the hell are you bellowing about?" It pissed him off to see Leland still sitting by the window where Kurt had left him earlier, his hair disheveled, his face flushed as he glared at poor Cory.

"He," Leland jabbed a finger at his aide, "says you called off my home therapy visits. That true?"

"We discussed this, Dad," he answered, struggling for calm. "You're well enough to go in for therapy. Tamara has more equipment and resources at the clinic to help get you back on your feet than here."

"And I told you I'm not leaving the ranch," he shot back without an explanation.

"Why? Everyone knows about your stroke, it's not as if anyone who sees you rolling into the clinic will be surprised. You need to get out of this…" Kurt flung his hand toward Brittany's shrine, "mausoleum." There, it was out. The wedge between them that was still keeping them apart.

A stricken look crossed Leland's face, one Kurt couldn't recall witnessing before. Shifting his bleak expression from Brittany's picture back out the window, he said in a quiet subdued tone, "Go have lunch. I'll think about therapy."

Kurt saw Cory's shoulders relax and nodded at him. It was a small boon, but it was progress. "Come into the kitchen and join me. You haven't taken a meal with me since I returned." He shoved aside the pang of hurt that wrought.

Instead of snapping in annoyance, his voice conveyed sad resignation that both frustrated and saddened Kurt as Leland replied, "No, go away, son."

"I'll get your tray, Mr. Wilcox." Cory followed Kurt out, saying, "Don't give up. He's changed since you've returned, but he's wrestling with something I can't get out of him."

"I've noticed the change, but I've also seen the surliness I've come to expect. He blows hot and cold." Slapping him on the back as they reached the kitchen, Kurt said, "You deserve a raise. Let me look at the books…"

Cory shook his head. "Thank you, but your dad just gave me a hefty pay increase. Yeah," he added when Kurt's eyes widened in surprise, "caught me off guard too."

In the past, Kurt always had to go to battle for wage increases and charitable contributions as Leland tended to hoard his money close. He always won the battles, but he'd never known his father to increase anyone's salary out of the blue, on his own, no matter how deserving. "So, another change we'll have to consider. At least it's a good one."

"Oh, it was very good." He didn't ask, but Cory's wide smile proved how pleased he was with it.

"There you two are." Babs pulled a large bowl out of the refrigerator. "Come have some potato salad and meatloaf. I was just getting ready to fix Mr. Wilcox's tray."

"I'll be in after I shower, Babs. Thanks."

Now, Kurt pondered as he went to his room, stripped and stepped under the hot spray, if only he could talk his dad into picking up the pace on therapy, get one blonde haired woman with lonely blue eyes out of his head and get caught up on paperwork, things just might settle down into a pleasant routine around here.

"BYE, MS. COLLINS."

Leslie smiled down at her second grader who never failed to give her a hug on his way out to the bus. "See you tomorrow, Timothy." She ruffled his bright red hair, her heart turning over when he gave her a gapped-tooth grin and finger wave before scampering down the front steps of the school.

For most people, Wednesdays signaled hump day and the

downslide to the weekend they were looking forward to. She viewed mid-week as getting close to spending another weekend alone in self-imposed isolation and wrestling with her plaguing thoughts. Pivoting, she went back inside to gather up her take-home work, thinking for about the tenth time what a mistake it was to turn tail and leave before entering the club last weekend. The past four nights since, her dreams were not only invaded by a dominant stranger sharing her bed but taunted by her cowardice in being unable to get back into the groove of visiting her favorite social hangout.

I'll just keep going back until I get over this funk, she decided as she returned to her classroom and started pushing in chairs and straightening desks. A knock on the open door drew her attention and when she saw Alan coming in, she prayed it wasn't to ask her out again.

"Hey, how's your week going?" he asked, leaning a hip against her desk as she walked behind it.

"Good. How about yours?" Picking up the stack of papers she was taking home to grade, she reached down to grab her satchel.

"Here." He beat her to it, their fingers brushing. A fleeting flashback of the hot flush that had jolted her the moment Kurt's hands wrapped around her arms to assist her up from the side-walk shook Leslie. As usual, with Alan there was no spark, which was both sad and a relief. "A few of us are stopping in at Chelsea's on the way home. Care to join us?"

The hopeful expression on his face kept Leslie from accepting the invitation. "Thanks, but I have a lot to do and would rather go straight home. Maybe next time."

He shrugged but disappointment clouded his eyes. "Sure. Have a nice evening then."

Maybe I should request a move, Leslie thought as she watched Alan walk out and then locked up her desk. A new city, maybe in a different state might be what she needed to move forward without so many regrets. But as she drove to her apartment, she realized she would miss the familiarity of Billings and the teachers she worked with as much as she would miss visiting the club and the minimal socializing she'd allowed herself to enjoy. Speaking of which…

As soon as Leslie slid out of her car, Nan pulled into the slot next to her, beaming as she, Sydney, Tamara and Avery all converged on her. "What are you doing here?" Leslie asked, perplexed to see them in front of her apartment.

"I brought Chinese." Nan held up a large bag of take-out that smelled wonderful.

"And we each brought a bottle of wine." Sydney gripped a sacked bottle by the neck, the same as Tamara and Avery.

Tamara cocked her head toward Leslie's apartment. "Are you going to invite us in or did we make this trip for nothing?"

Flustered, pleased and curious, Leslie smiled. "Sorry. You just took me by surprise. Please, come in." Unlocking her door, she held it open, saying, "I don't have much room but we can squeeze around my table to eat. How'd you know I love Chinese?"

"We didn't." Nan set the large bag on the cozy round table in the corner. "But, really, who doesn't?"

"We can wait if you want to change and get comfy," Avery offered as Leslie laid her satchel of papers on a small desk next to her laptop.

"I would, thanks." She pointed to the cupboards next to the sink. "Plates and glasses are in there. Help yourself. I only have one set of wine glasses."

Sydney shooed her toward the bedroom. "That's all we need, now go get changed then come join us. We have questions."

That caused Leslie to stumble with wary nervousness, her jaw going rigid at the tenable position they didn't know they could put her in with too many personal questions. Before she could say anything, Tamara jumped in. "Don't worry, you can tell us to mind our own business and we'll still share the food and wine. We mostly want to make sure you're okay since you haven't visited the club in weeks." She flipped Nan a censoring glare. "When someone else stayed away without a word, it was to eventually learn she could have used her friends a lot sooner."

"Are you ever going to let me live that down?" Nan grumbled.

"No," Sydney, Tamara and Avery all replied in unison.

"Trust me, Leslie. It's much easier to either unload now or tell us to back off than to keep silent. Been there, done that," Nan quipped with a rueful look.

She knew enough about the months Nan was away to know the tall, slender brunette dropped contact with her closest friends until she'd returned to Willow Springs last May. Leslie also heard about the horrendous ordeal that had kept her gone and silent on the matter for so long. Seeing the difference in Nan now as opposed to when she'd first come back to the club, and remembering the scenes between her and Master Dan that had worked to get her over her fears, it was hard not to envy the woman she'd known the longest out of the group; not what she'd gone through, but the relationship that had born fruit from her trauma.

"I'll be right out," she mumbled, pivoting to dash into her room.

Leslie never expected such a considerate gesture from people she'd kept at arm's length since meeting them. Sydney and Avery had bonded as newcomers to the club, and the town of Willow Springs. Tamara returned to her father's ranch last year after living away for five years, and her and Nan's friendship dated back to their school days. Of the four, Leslie had known Nan the longest, having met her the first night she visited the club. But not once in those three years had Nan made such a friendly overture, nor had she. This combined attempt to reach out to her stirred up the longing to include others in her everyday life, to build relationships instead of always remaining on guard against establishing them too deeply.

Changing into a worn pair of jeans and tee shirt, she padded barefoot back out to the kitchen, a warmth filling her chest as she saw them sitting at her table covered with take-out containers and chit-chatting as if comfortable in her small apartment. Their unexpected presence and concerned overtures didn't change her circumstances, but, God, their well-meaning intentions produced such a much-needed good feeling.

"We found paper plates," Avery said as Leslie sat down. "No sense in leaving you with a stack of dirty dishes."

"I wouldn't mind, not in exchange for not having to cook dinner." She spooned a serving of sweet and sour chicken onto a plate. "I rarely fuss and this looks as good as it smells."

"Cooking for one sucks. I used to box up food from the restaurant I worked at in St. Louis before heading home so I wouldn't have to fix something for just myself the next day." Sydney passed the fried rice with a deft change of subject. "So what gives, Les? You haven't come out to The Barn in weeks. Is everything okay?"

As much as she appreciated their concern, she couldn't exactly say, *Leslie Collins isn't my real name and if this rich guy who vowed revenge on me for testifying against his murderous sons ever finds out where I'm at, it could put anyone close to me in jeopardy.*

"Hey." Nan reached over and squeezed her arm. "We don't mean to pry. I know we're not close, and always figured you had your reasons for keeping to yourself. Just tell us to back off and we will. Sometimes, it's enough to know there are people you can turn to if you ever need, or want to. That's all we're trying to do today."

The tenseness eased out of Leslie's shoulders as she nodded and then let her gaze scan the other three. "Thank you, all of you. I can tell you there are... issues I can't relate to anyone that prevent me from making personal commitments, but you're right. Knowing I can reach out if I'm ever free to do so means a lot. Almost," she added with a teasing grin, "as much as this food. This is the best Chinese I've ever eaten." She shoveled in a forkful of moo goo gai pan into her mouth as everyone relaxed.

"Speaking of the club, we have to tell you about the two new members. They are Hot with a capital H." Tamara sighed and fanned herself.

Leslie laughed. "I thought you only had eyes for Master Connor."

"My eyes are free to look their fill, but my heart has always belonged to my husband. And now that I know for sure I have his, there's no way I'll do anything except look."

A dreamy haze filled Avery's brown eyes. "And fantasize. *Sheesh*, one look at Doctor Mitchell Hoffstetter can conjure up a slew of steamy imaginings."

"Speaking of fantasies," Nan said, looking toward Leslie. "The guys are planning a masquerade night in a couple of weeks. Dan mentioned it, and said they were considering requiring the subs to come in costume but leaving it up to the Doms if they want to participate. I already have a few ideas in mind. If you decide to attend, I'm always up to coming to Billings to shop."

Sydney, Avery and Tamara were quick to chime in and a stirring of interest in the idea tickled Leslie's stomach. Since it was still a few weeks off, she had time to get her act together and stop the moping over circumstances beyond her control.

Talk turned to men, unforgettable scenes that produced those awesome orgasms Leslie had never experienced before exploring her interest in alternative sex. As she ate and listened to the banter going on around her table, her mind drifted to the stranger who had also wrung several off-the-chart climaxes from her perspiring, writhing body. She wondered if he ever thought of her, and if so, was it with pleasure or disbelief over her irresponsible decision to invite him into her home? She supposed it didn't matter now what he thought of her or those hours they spent together naked. The odds of them ever meeting again were virtually nil, and that was for the best.

It didn't take long after she thanked the girls again and said good-bye for the loneliness to creep in. An hour later, the silence of her apartment pressed down on her and she tried remedying that by turning on the television while she graded papers. But even the tin-canned laughter from sitcom reruns couldn't suppress the ache to talk and laugh with friends again.

It wasn't as if she'd spent the last three years in total seclusion, she thought with a surge of annoyance with herself. She'd enjoyed meeting her co-workers for drinks or lunch, and a few times she'd taken in a movie with her divorced neighbor upstairs. When Carl had pushed for more than a platonic evening of companionship, Leslie put a stop to those evenings out. It helped he remained friendly and was already seeing someone else.

Even though Billings was a fraction of the size of Reno with considerably fewer attractions and venues for entertainment, Leslie admitted there was a certain appeal to the slower paced, smaller town living, not to mention the scenic vistas of the surrounding mountain-backed prairies. She still found herself slowing on the highway when she spotted a herd of slow-moving, shaggy-haired bison or the streak of several graceful pronghorn antelope out across the meadows. Whenever these depressing moods would hit her in the past, all she had to do to dispel them was think about the positive aspects of the changes in her life or force herself to go out with acquaintances she enjoyed spending time with.

But those anecdotes failed to work this time around, pushing her into easing her despondency with a one-night stand. Just because that night had resulted in an awesome, unforgettable few hours didn't negate the risk she'd taken by making that rash decision, or convince her she should push her luck and try for a repeat with another stranger. She wasn't that desperate. Yet.

By the time Leslie climbed into bed, she'd decided to put out the effort to return to the club again as soon as she was certain she wouldn't turn tail and run just because others were lucky enough to have what she didn't, or ever could.

Four weeks later

Despite her resolve to get over her funk and move on, the month of September flew by before Leslie got around to returning to The Barn. With having several students this year who were struggling with learning disabilities, she'd taken up tutoring both after school and on Saturdays to help them keep up. Then her car's transmission went out and she wasn't prepared for the hefty repair bill. Instead of tacking on to her unexpected expense by renting a vehicle for the week hers was in the shop, she hitched rides to school with another teacher and stayed home over the weekend. The following week was the school's open house and fun night and after that an allergic reaction to something she ate laid her up for yet another weekend. During all that, Sydney, Avery, Tamara and Nan had taken turns sending her a short text at the end of each week, keeping the message to simple 'will we see you this week?' or 'hope you can make it tonight' comments that helped keep her thoughts on the positive side and her spirits up.

Before she knew it, the first weekend in October was upon her with nothing to keep her from driving out to the club. After answering Nan's text and confirming she would see her this weekend at the club, Nan reminded her about masquerade night. Reading Nan's response drew a smile from Leslie and boosted her confidence in being able to return without selfish ill-feelings getting her down.

Woo hoo! Can't wait to see you and fill you in on what you've missed!

Us girls plan to gather at my old apartment above the tea shop beforehand to disguise ourselves, hopefully good enough to make the Doms work at guessing who's who. Feel free to join us – 7:00.

Before Leslie could come up with an excuse, she sent a quick reply telling her she would be there. She'd never ventured into Willow Springs, but Nan's directions to her tea shop were easy enough, and she figured meeting up with them first would keep her from bolting at the last minute like she'd done a few weeks ago. Shopping for a costume would be fun and would occupy her mind and time, hopefully enough to keep her from second-guessing her decision.

"WHAT THE HELL was that thing you unloaded from the horse trailer?"

Kurt's pleasure at seeing his father out on the porch for a change instead of at his bedroom window took a nosedive as soon as Leland opened his mouth. Taking off his hat, he slapped it against his thigh, annoyed with his derogatory tone and question. "I know Roy gave you my message when I called to have him clear one of the smaller corrals for the wild mustang I purchased, and you knew I was going to auction today."

Leland nodded with a scowl. "But not to buy that nag. For God's sake, Kurt, that animal is skin and bones, and nasty to boot. What are you going to do with him?"

"I could say the same about you," he shot back. The past month had yielded little changes in Leland's health and attitude, but not enough as far as Kurt was concerned. It had taken three weeks before his father admitted defeat in getting him to relent on resuming the private therapy sessions. Just this past week, he'd allowed Cory to drive him into the clinic and had returned tired but with a healthy flush covering his face that Kurt was pleased to see. The bad news was he'd only exercised enough in the weeks before that to keep from losing ground, doing nothing to improve his strength and mobility. "As you know, the stallion was headed to the dog food factory and I couldn't let that happen. He's young, mean as a snake and malnourished, but I can see his will to live in his eyes, along with his intelligence. He'll be worth the effort to nurse him back to health, maybe even tame him."

Leland snorted in disbelief. "I thought you knew horseflesh better than that. That's what you get for wasting your time behind a desk in Houston for so long."

"Well I'm not in Houston anymore and I still know a good horse when I see one." Yanking open the door, he looked over his shoulder and caught Leland glancing around at him, an undefinable gleam in his eyes. "What?" he asked, wondering at the softening around his mouth.

"Nothing. Go on. You don't want to be late gettin' to that club of yours. I have plenty of time to tell you I told you so."

Shaking his head, Kurt headed to his bathroom thinking he wasn't he only one who could use the relief from a long, vigorous fucking. He'd never hidden his sexual proclivities from Leland, but also had never discussed them openly. He was Kurt's father, and some things didn't change no matter how old either of them got. Noting the time was later than he'd thought, he rushed through a shower and dinner before driving out to The Barn looking forward to masquerade night. With any luck, he would finally hook up with someone who could make him forget one night over five weeks ago and one woman whose memory refused to stay in the back of his mind, where he'd delegated all the others who had come before her.

After making two trips into Billings and taking the time to stop by Leslie's apartment only to find her not at home, he'd given up. He knew what her breathy moans sounded like when she was aroused, how soft her skin felt, how tightly her hot, slick pussy gripped his fingers and cock and could still vividly recall the despondency that had clouded her pretty blue eyes. Other than that, he knew nothing about the woman who left such a lasting impact on him. Vowing to put an end to his concern for her tonight, he entered the club in time to catch the last half of the monthly business meeting with the Masters before the doors opened to the rest of the members.

All six of his closest friends, owners of the club and Masters were congregated around the bar, laughing as Kurt entered the playroom. Looking forward to an evening of socializing and tormenting a willing submissive, he strode toward the group vowing not to let thoughts of his father or a desperate stranger intrude on his fun.

Chapter 5

"No one is going to recognize you in that outfit," Nan said as she took in Leslie's ankle-length white sheath dress cinched around the waist with a wide, gold belt. "When you put it all together with the fancy head piece, matching arm bands and black wig, it's easy to guess you're Cleopatra, but with the mask and heavily made-up eyes, even I can barely recognize your face."

"It won't matter if I can get the attention of one of the new Doms you told me about since I'll still be a stranger to them." The thought of hooking up with someone new tonight appealed to Leslie. With luck, she could put one stranger out of her mind for good with another. The new members, a doctor who had relocated to Willow Springs from Denver and a wealthy cattleman who had just returned home after living in Texas for several years, sounded interesting. Although, given the jolt she experienced upon hearing Master Wilcox's first name was Kurt, the same as her one-night-stand stranger, she might avoid him just to keep from making unwanted comparisons.

"Tell me some more about Masters Greg and Devin's new sub," she prodded, taking a seat on the couch while she and Nan waited for Sydney, Avery and Tamara to emerge from the bedroom. She was still struggling to wrap her head around Nan's engagement, trying to picture the independent, confirmed bachelorette giving up her cozy apartment above her quaint tea shop to move out to Dan's small ranch, and now she'd learned the hot Doms who loved ménage scenes recently joined the ranks of committed members. So far, Leslie had managed to stifle the pang of regret she had experienced when each of the others had pledged fidelity to one person, but that might not last when she saw the two Masters with their new submissive.

Nan arranged the deep red satin folds of her saloon girl costume around her legs as she sat in the armchair facing the couch. "She's really nice. It's fun to watch them together. Kelsey is only an inch or two over five foot, small boned with big blue eyes and almost white hair. Her fey appearance doesn't keep her from giving as good as she gets when either Greg or Devin pushes her buttons."

"You must be talking about Kelsey." Sydney padded into the room wearing a peasant dress, the see-through, lacy white bodice revealing her unfettered breasts and dusky nipples. "She's my kind of girl."

"That's because she's so much like you," Avery chimed in from behind her, her abundant curves spilling out of the tight, skimpy, bright green bra that matched the sheer, billowing, hip-hugging pants of her harem outfit.

Sydney smirked. "I knew there was a reason I liked her so much."

"Oh my God," Nan breathed, coming to her feet as Tamara joined them decked out in a body-molding, bright fuchsia, latex cat suit. With the front zipper lowered to her waist, the plump fullness of her breasts drew the eye as much as the noticeable peeks of bare flesh under the mesh. "I have to know where you got that."

Flushing, Tamara tossed her long black hair with a wide

smile. "Think Connor will know it's me?" She held her mask up to her eyes by the long handle.

"Yes. In that outfit, there's no hiding your baby bump," Sydney drawled, resting a hand on her own stomach.

Baby? Leslie's gaze swung from admiring Tamara's three-inch heels to her waist and then over to Sydney's less obvious little bulge behind her loose skirt. Living with a target on her back prevented her from even thinking about having children some day and there was no stopping or ignoring the painful twist of exclusion cramping her abdomen. Forcing a smile of congratulations, she hurried over to give each of them a hug.

"I'm so happy for you both. This is what I get for staying away for so long. It'll take me all night to get caught up with everyone."

"Just be sure to save time to play." Nan opened the door and waved everyone out. "No offense, Leslie, but you look like you could use a long session with an attentive Dom."

"You know, I think that's exactly what I need." They traipsed downstairs and Leslie waved as she opened her car door. "See you there." Settling behind the wheel, she waited until they pulled out before following them.

The charm of Willow Springs' business square had struck Leslie when she'd driven past the century-old buildings that still housed the city offices and library on her way in. Quaint gift shops, a local diner and a center fountain squared off by towering pines made her wish she'd taken the time to visit sooner. With her new resolution to move forward and put herself out more, she made a silent promise to return soon, take Nan up on her offer of tea in her shop and check out the arts and crafts in the display windows along the covered sidewalks.

Turning off the highway onto the narrow lane leading to the club, Leslie sucked in a deep breath, vowing to get back into the groove of enjoying herself in the only way she'd found that eased the stress of keeping her true identity a secret. Just in case she wanted to bail early though, she opted for a parking space at the rear of the already crowded gravel lot. Checking her wig in the mirror, she slipped on her mask, a flutter of excitement winging through her with the thought of submitting in disguise to a new Dom. Given her previous response to a stranger, she was all for a repeat with another man she didn't know any better than he knew her.

Leslie's friends were already inside by the time she entered the foyer and stowed her shoes in a cubby. The two-stepping beat of a country western tune seeped through the door leading into the social hall. She'd watched members skilled in line dancing move in sync on the dance floor numerous times but never got up the nerve to join in. Her blood warmed as she entered the cavernous space and took in the activity already taking place, the two hours spent with the girls having helped put away her misplaced envy over their good fortune.

She paused a moment to get her bearings and reacclimate to seeing everyone again. Delightful ripples of excitement tingled under her skin as faint echoes of slapping flesh and soft cries emanating from the loft reached her ears while she caught sight of the arousal-stirring play going on around the tables. Spotting Sue Ellen already draped over her husband's lap, his hand resting on her bare butt, sent a wave of heat straight down between Leslie's legs. Clenching her own buttocks in response to the remembered pain of a hard spanking that always led to a more intense orgasm, she now questioned how she'd gone so long without getting those needs met. Padding across the wood floor trying to figure out who was who behind the disguises and enjoying the probing, scrutinizing looks from Doms who couldn't pinpoint her identity, one thing became abundantly clear – wallowing in self-pity for close to two months had been a colossal waste of time.

Stopping at the bar, she held her breath as Caden, Sydney's husband came strolling over, waiting to see if he recognized her.

Nudging his Stetson back, he subjected her to a detailed scrutiny while holding a hand out for her drink card.

"Nice getup and you look familiar, so I know you're a regular. What can I get you?"

"A beer, please." Handing him the card, Leslie relaxed until his blue eyes lit with recognition.

Snapping his fingers, Caden smiled, saying, "Leslie, how the hell are you, darlin'?"

She returned his smile, warmed by his welcome. "I'm good, Sir. Was it my voice, or something else?"

Popping off the bottle cap, he squeezed the brew into a koozie, handed it over and then flicked the end of her wig. "Your voice and those baby blues. If you hadn't stayed away from us for so long I might have recognized you sooner. It's good to see you here again."

"It's good to be back, Sir," she returned, surprised at how quickly that true statement had come about. "Thanks for the drink."

"You're welcome. We have a good turnout. Have fun tonight, and don't be a stranger." Winking, he left to serve someone else.

That was the plan, Leslie thought, sliding off the stool. Before joining the unattached subs in the sitting area waiting to catch the eye of a Master, she veered toward the dance floor to watch for a few minutes. Standing off to the side with the other onlookers, she wasn't the only one who found it amusing to see women dressed in costumes doing the two-step alongside men wearing the usual attire for country-western dancing of tight jeans and boots, a few still wearing their Stetsons. Her gaze swept from the back row to the front and she recognized all the Doms until her eyes landed on the taut, denim-covered buttocks and broad shoulders of the man with his back to her in the front row. Even if she couldn't see his face, she would've remembered any Dom who could gyrate and swivel his hips with such eye-catching, pussy-dampening talent. God, could he move, and she wondered if he was one of the new members.

Leslie damn near drooled as he two-stepped into giving her a side view of his sexy hip action that drew her nipples into stiff peaks. Dragging her eyes away from his pelvis, she caught her first glimpse of his face and stiffened at the familiarity of his dark, rugged profile. And then he executed another shuffle of his feet with knees bent, his pelvis circling in a way that pulled her gaze back down. The rhythmic rolls of his crotch conjured up an image of down and dirty fucking that prompted her to tighten her thighs to contain her response before she dared to look up again. When she did, she went cold with a shockwave of instant, face-to-face recognition. There was no mistaking the sexy Dom standing just yards in front of her, even with his black Stetson shielding his eyes, was the same Kurt as her one-night stand all those weeks ago.

What were the odds? she bemoaned as she gathered her frayed nerves and spun around before he recognized her. Leslie was halfway to the door before she slowed her hasty retreat and dared to peek around a small group of people and back at the dance floor. Her taut muscles slowly relaxed as she saw he hadn't skipped a beat in dancing and wasn't coming after her. *He didn't recognize me as Cleopatra.* With the relief came a sudden, titillating idea. Could she work him out of her system and put an end to the plaguing dreams of their one time together by indulging in another night of anonymous sex? From the uncomfortable dampness coating her thong, she couldn't deny watching him had stirred her up. She already knew she would respond to him, how good a Dom he was. If she concentrated on getting her needs met, of submitting to his dominance and relieving the ache that had been building since she'd seen Kurt last, she believed she could keep from revealing her identity.

With her heart pounding from the risk but still unable to walk away from this second chance, Leslie pivoted and had only taken four steps back toward the dance floor when she spotted Master Kurt walking toward her. Now holding his hat, the midnight eyes she remembered so well showed interest but not a hint of surprised recognition, bolstering her courage.

———

SEEING a sexy Cleopatra look-alike eying him with a wide gaze, bare toes curled against the wood floor and taut nipples had drawn Kurt's interest in a sub for the first time that night. The white toga-style dress draped over her curves emphasized the fullness of her breasts, every bump of her rigid nubs outlined against the soft material. When she'd executed an abrupt turn-around and walked away, he'd made the snap decision to snatch her up before another Dom beat him to her.

Now, standing close enough to see her eyes were as blue as the Montana sky in summer and the shape of her face tugging at his memory banks, he wondered if she was someone he'd played with here before.

"You're staring, Sir."

The hint of accusation in her pert tone amused him. Kurt didn't mind when his habit of silently sizing up a potential partner for the evening rubbed a sub the wrong way. He didn't want someone who would let him walk all over her; just who would not only bow to his dominance, but relish whatever he tormented her with.

"Yes, I am. I'm Master Kurt. You make a lovely Cleopatra."

"Thank you." A small smile curved her soft lips. "I enjoyed watching you dance."

Even her voice rang bells and prompted him to look closer at her features below the mask. Wanting to know more about her, he replied, "And I would enjoy getting to know you better. Are you free to join me upstairs?" A cock-stirring spark lit her eyes and his quick, uncharacteristic infatuation grew. Holding out his hand, he said, "Let's sit while you finish your beer. I could be wrong, but you look familiar. Have we paired up before tonight?"

She tugged on his hand, halting him before he took a step toward the nearest empty table. "I'd rather go straight up, if it's all the same with you."

The flash of need that wiped away the spark and was, he suspected, the cause of her rash decision struck another chord of familiarity in him. "*Do* we know each other, sweetheart?"

Her palm turned clammy under his, and her entire arm went rigid at his simple inquiry. She shifted her gaze off to the side, a telltale sign of evasiveness that triggered more suspicions.

"No, Sir." She looked back at him with a crooked smile. "I haven't been here in a few weeks, but to be honest, a few of the other girls mentioned you in a very good way."

"I'm flattered, but it would help if you'd tell me your name." Kurt cupped her elbow and led her toward the stairs, adding, "Your real name."

"But that will ruin the fun of remaining anonymous. Isn't that part of the lure that prompted the Masters to plan this masquerade night?"

She had a point, he conceded, but he was ninety-nine percent sure he knew her from somewhere and was starting to suspect she didn't want him to know that. Why, he couldn't fathom. As they reached the loft with its dimmer lighting, reverberating soft cries and straining moans accompanying snaps against bare flesh, several ideas ran through his head on how to pull the truth from her.

Facing her, he asked, "Any hard limits or an apparatus you want me to stay away from?"

"Light pain only, I'm good with any bondage and the standard color codes for safewords," she rambled off, as if she wanted to hurry this along. He had news for her; he wasn't the hurry sort.

Yanking her up against him, the rigid tips of her breasts

pressed against his chest, her startled gasp changing to a sigh as he covered her mouth with his. Kurt meant to go slow, to savor those soft lips and her quivering body aligned with his. But she parted her mouth without urging, accepted the thrust and exploration of his tongue with welcoming enthusiasm and shivered with a low, vibrating moan when he nipped her plump, lower lip. Crushing his mouth on hers, he filled his hands with her malleable buttocks and brought her pelvis tight against his, her soft pubis a nice cushion for his hard cock. By the time he pulled back, he was more than ready to move this along.

"Come on." Grasping her hand, he led her toward the chain stations along the back wall. Halfway across the spacious loft, he paused at the wooden A-frame and turned to ask if she'd ever tried the newest addition to the bondage equipment. Instead, he caught her gazing at Grayson's tender expression as he released Avery from the St. Andrew's cross, the fleeting look of longing crossing her face sending a shock wave of instant recognition through Kurt. There was no mistaking that expression, or where he'd seen it before.

What were the odds of the same Leslie he'd rescued from a mugging and then ended up in her bed being a submissive member of The Barn? Maybe not such a longshot as he recalled her willing compliance to his commands that night and that this was the closest club to Billings. Since he assumed she recognized him, he wondered what game she was playing and refused to let her get away with keeping her true identity from him. After that night, she should know she could trust him, and it didn't sit well that she didn't.

With a determined yank on her hand, he strolled over to the nearest dangling chain. "Know why I like this option best?" he asked, flicking the cuffs attached to the end of the metal links.

"No, why?" She bit her lip as he removed the fancy gold belt around her waist, tossing it on a bench against the wall.

"It gives me unfettered access to your whole body." With his eyes on hers, gauging her every reaction, Kurt tugged the ties at her shoulders and the white garment dropped to her feet. "Very pretty." He brushed his knuckles over her turgid nipples, enjoying the way they puckered tighter, proving his memory was spot on from their previous night together. Running the tips of his fingers down her abdomen to hook into the skinny straps of her thong, he asked, "On or off?"

She clutched his upper arms, her nails digging into his skin as she said, "I'm good with taking it off."

That answered one question, Kurt mused as he slid the satin scrap of material down her long smooth legs. Alcohol wasn't responsible for her boldness and uninhibitedness with him the last time he got her naked. It appeared that enticing trait came naturally to her. Bending to scoop up the dress and thong put his face right in front of her puffy, denuded folds, the dampness coating her slit a hard-to-resist temptation that drew him forward. One slow lick up her seam was enough to remember the taste of her, one lap over her smooth labia enough to reacquaint himself with the shape and softness of her flesh. Her hands clutched on his shoulders, where she kept them as he straightened and flung her clothes on top of the belt. He left the fancy headdress and arm bands on, liking the naked pagan goddess look of her as he gripped her wrists and attached the cuffs.

"I like how agreeable you are, how you don't shy away from what you're comfortable with. You remind me of someone else I met not long ago." It was difficult not to smile as her hands jerked in his before he pulled the chain up, enjoying toying with her.

"I'd rather you think of me instead of someone else right now," she returned tartly. "Sir."

"Well, I admit it's not becoming to mention someone else but rest assured, sweetheart, you have my full attention and my thoughts are of no one else but you. I need to get a few things from the prop cabinet."

Kurt could feel her eyes on him as he retrieved a spreader bar from the items available for everyone to use. He started to shut the cabinet door when he spotted the spiked five-wheel pinwheel and remembering her responses to his butt slaps and nipple pinches, he decided to add something extra to his hands and mouth this time around.

She gave the pinwheel a wary look when he returned. "Uh, I'm not sure…"

"Give me a color," he snapped, refusing to let her slide on that issue.

Jerking from his hard tone, Leslie stuttered, "Oh, um, yellow."

Tucking the pinwheel handle into his back pocket, he nudged her feet apart with one booted foot. "What are you unsure about? This?" Kurt held up the bar and she frowned in annoyance. He shouldn't find that look amusing, but given the circumstances, he did.

"No. I've used those before," she huffed. "But not that spiky thing."

"Then save yellow for when that comes into play, or anything else you're not sure of." Squatting down, he cuffed her ankles to the bar then trailed his palms up the inside of her legs as he rose. Stopping at her upper thighs, he dug his fingers into the muscles and dipped his thumbs between her labia. Warm, slick wetness coated the pads of his thumbs as her hips jutted forward.

"Tell me, just so I'm clear," he murmured, running his lips up the side of her neck as he inched further inside her pussy, "you said anything except harsh pain, correct?"

"Yes, yes… *please*," she gasped, thrusting her pelvis into his hands again.

"So, sex with a virtual stranger isn't a problem?" he taunted, circling her clit with one thumb while stroking the soft tissues lining her inner muscles with the other. He almost chuckled as she jerked with a harsh, indrawn breath. Was she wondering if he suspected her true identity, or just remembering the last time he had her naked and writhing?

MAYBE THIS WASN'T such a good idea. Leslie speculated about pleading a case of lust induced insanity to rationalize why she'd accepted Master Kurt's invitation without telling him who she was. Did that last question mean he recognized her, or was it just a teasing innuendo, like it sounded? Either way, she needed to decide fast – say red or answer him. As he pulled his hands away from her, the loss of his touch left her desperate for more, settling the decision.

"This is a safe club, and you wouldn't be a Master here if I couldn't trust you."

"That is true, so how about we get to know each other better by testing your boundaries? Close your eyes and keep them shut."

Leslie noticed Master Grayson taking over as monitor as Master Kurt reached into his back pocket for the spiked pinwheel that had sent a ripple of unease crawling under her skin upon first seeing it. Obeying his order, she lowered her lids and found a measure of comfort in shutting off her vision. She enjoyed the heat and discomfort from a spanking and the sting from the snap of a flogger, but had never experienced the sharp, needle-like pricks from one of the medical instruments some liked to play with. Holding her breath, she braced for that deeper pain but he surprised her by lightly rolling the pointed wheel down the ticklish underside of her raised right arm. Instead of pressing the sharp spikes into her skin, the slow glide scraped just enough to titillate and arouse an ache for more.

"Not so bad, is it?" he asked, his breath warm against her neck as he switched to her other arm.

"No, at least not yet." He was a Dom, so, while she trusted

him with her safety, she wasn't foolish enough to think those light caresses were all he had in mind for her. His amused voice confirmed her suspicions.

"Smart girl, at least in some areas." Cupping her breast with his free hand, he brushed a thumb across her nipple.

Leslie could sense his black eyes on her as Master Kurt scraped the pinwheel over the fleshy underside of her other breast next, applying more pressure as his nail scratched across her nipple. She squeezed her eyes to keep from opening them against the sudden tiny pricks of pain that elicited a spurt of cream between her legs. His deep, throaty chuckle in her ear sent shivers up and down her writhing body, a response she could remember all too clearly from the last time they were together.

"I think you like this little toy. I know I do. Or, maybe it's how you respond, no matter what I do that I'm enjoying so much." Satisfaction laced his voice as he rolled the tormenting toy down her waist, his other hand sliding from her breast around her back and down to her butt.

A cry spilled from her mouth as a stinging swat heated her right cheek the same time those sharp points pressed into the sensitive flesh above her pubis. Leslie rocked her hips against the dual attack, unsure whether she was embracing the discomfort or fighting against it. "Sir, please," she whispered, her thighs tensing with the graze of those rough fingertips between her buttocks, over her anus and down to her wet slit. She was so close to that lovely zone where nothing mattered but the pleasure taking over her body and mind; to being in that comforting place where she could briefly forget the cruel death of a decent man for no other reason than two privileged teens getting their kicks. For weeks she'd been aching for that temporary reprieve from what witnessing that heartbreaking scene had cost her, and Master Kurt was proving as good at taking over her senses as she remembered.

"Please, what, sweetheart? More of this?" Another smack

seared her left cheek. "Or this?" He rolled the pinwheel up and down her inner thigh, leaving a trail of throbbing pinpricks behind, the unpleasant pain quickly morphing into pulsing pleasure. "Or maybe you're ready for more of this." One finger pressed up inside her pussy, her inner muscles clamping around the invading digit in a desperate attempt to hold him there.

"I don't know," Leslie admitted, wishing he would just get her off in silence. The constant questioning kept her on edge as much as keeping her eyes closed and trying to guess where he would go next.

"Then let's try an easier question." Kurt tugged on her clit and bit her nipple as he asked, "What do you do for a living?"

The question took Leslie by surprise, pulling her back from the building euphoria for a moment. They hadn't exchanged any personal information about each other that night and she figured it wouldn't hurt to reveal one personal tidbit, especially if it got her closer to orgasm. "I teach grade school, second grade."

"I can picture you doing that, and your students loving you." He deepened his voice, inserting more demand as he raked the spikes across one buttock and thrust up into her. "Are you going to tell me where we've met before?"

Leslie's eyes flew open, her heart leaping into her throat as her buttocks clenched and her pussy spasmed. The hazy fog of arousal lifted enough for her to worry and frown at him as she insisted, "I told you, we haven't met here before."

Dropping the pinwheel, Master Kurt gripped her butt cheek. "Anywhere else?" Two blows in rapid succession inflamed her buttocks as he stretched her sheath by adding two more fingers, his thrusts abrading her swollen, needy clit.

Shaking her head against the onslaught, she gasped, "No!" and closed her eyes again, afraid he would see the truth behind the lie.

Disappointment swamped Kurt after hoping Leslie would come clean about her identity. How could she think he wouldn't remember her? He remembered everything; her body was just as soft and receptive to his touch and commands, her expressions and voice just as desperate and needy, her blue eyes just as sad behind the swirling, dilated arousal. There were some things the mask and wig couldn't disguise.

He had wanted to fuck her again, ached to slide his throbbing cock into the slick wet heat clutching at his fingers, but given her continued subterfuge, he would refrain. He couldn't leave her hurting though. If it was only a physical release she was needing, he could easily walk away as punishment for her lies. But her obvious emotional pain tugged at him, just like the night she'd gotten drunk as a means to cope with whatever issues were plaguing her. Later, he intended to delve into what it was about this one woman that pulled at him more than any other, but right now he had a duty, and a desire to ease the emotional strain etched on her face and clouding her eyes.

"Then there's no reason to leave you hanging, is there, sweetheart?" He had the pleasure of seeing her blanch before he set up a rhythm alternating deep thrusts inside her quivering pussy with hip-jarring smacks on her soft buttocks. The velvet soft muscles gripped his fingers as he jabbed deep enough to bring her to her toes while her ass turned hot under his hand. The swat he delivered as he pulled his fingers back drew a whimpering cry and pushed her pelvis forward to press against his palm. Three more times he plunged inside her liquid heat, rasping the swollen tissues of her clit and convulsing pussy while caressing her warmed buttocks and then withdrawing and landing a blistering spank on the bouncing globes.

"*Yes*, God, please, *yes*," she mewled over and over, her perspiration-slick body undulating in the restraints as he plundered and smacked until she convulsed with a spate of cream and tight clutches around his pummeling fingers. Laying her head back, her cry rent the space around them, drew heads and grins and had Kurt's own heart aching at the sobbing relief in her strident voice.

By the time he brought her down from the exultant high and released her to fall into his arms, he knew he wasn't done with her. It was more than curiosity at this point that made him decide to find the answers to what made her tick, what prodded her into taking a stranger home one night and then lie to a Master weeks later. He accepted the subbie blanket Grayson handed him without a word, wrapped it around her quivering body and held her close while the tremors still running through her body slowly eased and her breathing returned to normal. When they did, he leaned back and nudged her chin up with two fingers.

Kurt waited for Leslie's eyes to clear and focus on him, but as soon as she came to her senses, she pulled back, both physically and mentally.

"I… thank you, Sir. I have a long drive home, so I think I should go now."

He wasn't surprised at her withdrawal, in fact had been expecting it. "Let me help you dress and walk you out, then." He released her to pick up her dress and panties.

"I can do it, I don't need help," she insisted, her voice husky.

"I'm sure you can and that you don't, but you're getting my help anyway. If you argue, you'll find your ass over a spanking bench." He smirked, reached around and patted her hot butt. "Think you'll like getting a few strokes of my belt in the next few minutes?"

Her jaw went taut and those blue eyes behind the mask flared with irritation, but her pouty nipples tightened and goosebumps popped up along her arms, the two responses at odds with each other. "No, Sir, I don't think I would."

"That's what I thought." She might enjoy a session with his belt some other time, but he could tell she was done for tonight.

Leslie dressed quickly, as if eager to be on her way, or to get away from him, Kurt wasn't sure which. By the time he took her hand and escorted her out to her car, he decided to send her off with something to think about before they met again. And, they *would* meet up again. Opening her car door, he waited until she slid behind the wheel and looked up at him, reaching for the handle.

Leaning down, he gave her a quick, hard kiss before backing up, saying, "See you soon, Leslie." He shut the door and strolled back inside, grinning from the shock on her pale face.

Chapter 6

Leslie spent all day Sunday reeling from Kurt's admission of knowing her true identity last night. She awoke with the effects of that scene still lingering, the soreness where he'd pressed the pinwheel hardest and the tenderness of her butt every time she sat down. It wasn't the hardest spanking she'd ever received, but the most memorable as it had contributed to another intense climax. The heights she'd reached with him were beyond her imagination; nothing had felt that good and because of that, she was still shaken today. How one man managed to get such a tight grip on her in one night and maintain that hold for weeks until they met up again she couldn't understand, let alone ever thought possible. And now she was left wondering and worrying what he meant by 'seeing her again'. Maybe it had been naïve to believe he wouldn't see through her disguise, but how was she to know he would remember a one-night stand weeks later?

Putting on music, Leslie went through the routine of cleaning her apartment even though it didn't need it. With it being just her living in the small space, it didn't get dirty enough to do a thorough cleaning every week, but it was a habit she'd gotten into when she'd owned a house in Reno and the mindless tasks were a way to unwind from the hours she'd spent at the club.

The one good thing she could attribute to being uprooted from her home and given a new identity was the freedom she'd gained to explore the BDSM lifestyle that had intrigued her for years. She could never get up the nerve to attend a beginner's night at one of the clubs in Reno, fearing those closest to her would find out and turn judgmental. Here, she wasn't close enough to anyone to worry about what they thought of her. Once she'd discovered the stress-relief benefits of sexual submission, she joined the club and prayed wind of her involvement never reached the ears of her co-workers at school. It wasn't until her introduction to alternative sex and her embracement of her submissive side that she'd felt a kinship with other regular members at The Barn, and eventually grown to crave more from those limited relationships.

Leslie ran the vacuum around the couch, her mind conjuring up the image of her lying under Kurt, her body bowing to his demands as she writhed in the pleasure he'd proven so good at unleashing both that night and last night. In the weeks since she'd invited him home with her, she had failed to find an answer as to why she couldn't put him and that night out of her mind. Now she found herself questioning how she could have been so stupid as to risk indulging in another scene thinking he wouldn't remember her.

"It doesn't matter," she muttered, stowing the vacuum in the hall closet. If she stayed away from the club, she wouldn't see him again, and that would be that. Her stomach cramped at the thought of once again giving up the only social and sexual outlet she'd allowed herself in the last three years. But what choice did she have? *Master* Kurt would demand answers and explanations if she returned next week, and she didn't have any to give him, not without revealing her enrollment in the Witness Protection program. That was the one thing Detective Reynolds had drilled into her as he and Agent Summers laid out the details of her relocation – never reveal her real name or the circumstances that had forced her to change it. In this day and age of advanced technology and computer savvy techs willing to do anything for the right amount of money, it was too easy for Edwin Glascott to use his wealth and influence to track her down, not to mention to hire someone to do his dirty work for him.

The break-in at her house following the trial was solved, but there was no mistaking the threat when a car drove by the next day, the driver taking aim and shooting as soon as she'd opened her front door. Leslie still broke out in a cold sweat when she recalled the loud rapport of gun fire and her neighbor's painful exclamation and shocked face as the eighty-something man's arm was grazed. Even though the injury was superficial, it forced her hand into accepting witness protection. There was no way she'd risk someone else's safety, or her own.

Leslie finished lunch and then booted up her computer to go over the week's lesson plans, hoping work would keep her from thinking about a black-eyed cowboy who could turn her into a hot mess of longing with just one searing look. She managed to get finished in an hour, making a note of which students still needed help in some areas, and then spent an hour in the apartment complex's gym, working out the last of the soreness from her physical exertion last night. Two months abstinence from the club activities left her out of shape for the intense scene Master Kurt put her through.

Returning to her apartment, she allowed a satisfied smile to curve her lips as she admitted the orgasms he'd wrung from her were worth the discomfort after weeks of inaction. As soon as she shut and locked the door behind her, her phone rang and she dug it out of her bag. Her throat went dry upon seeing Detective

Reynolds' name displayed and well-remembered ripples of misgiving trickled through her. Once a month, Agent Cathy Summers from the Witness Protection program checked in with her, but she hadn't heard from the detective in charge of Alessandro Carmichael's murder since right before she was flown to Montana.

Leaning against the door for support, she pressed the button to answer. "Detective. It's been a while."

"Yes, and I'm sorry to contact you out of the blue like this, but I wanted to be the one to tell you the Glascott brothers were in a knife fight at the prison last night. Jason was killed and Jake is in critical condition along with two other inmates. None of them are expected to make it," he said, his tone carrying a hint of worry.

Leslie closed her eyes as she recalled the Glascotts' cold faces right before Jake shot Alessandro in the head. She didn't understand why her abdomen tightened with guilt or why her heart turned over in sympathy for how their young lives ended. They were evil, neither showing an ounce of remorse for the horrible act they'd committed, just nerve-racking hatred toward her in the courtroom.

"I'm sorry. You don't think I should be happy about this, do you?"

"No, but I'm giving you a heads-up. Edwin Glascott is on a rampage. He's been fighting tooth and nail to get both boys' convictions overturned or, barring that, a new trial. I want you to be aware of what's going on. You're safe where you're at as long as you don't tell anyone who you really are."

"I haven't. I'd say pass on my condolences, but I don't think that would go over well with the family. Thank you for letting me know."

He hesitated then said, "Take care, Leslie, and remember, you did the right thing, a good thing."

"Yeah, I'll do that." Leslie hung up, wishing doing the right thing wasn't always so damn hard.

KURT LEANED his forearms on the top rail of the corral, chewing on a blade of straw as he watched the mustang pace back and forth along the opposite side. The stallion couldn't understand why he was confined when there was all that open space for him to run and enjoy. He figured the animal had suffered worse than being penned up and hoped six months from now, the horse would know he only had his best interest at heart. It would take at least that long to put the weight back on him. For the next few weeks, his plan, other than nutrition, was to simply get the mustang used to his presence and let him know no one here would hurt him.

In time, he would discover what made the stallion tick, just as he was determined to unearth what had driven Leslie to invite a stranger home with her and prompted her to lie about her identity last night. Her eyes portrayed the same desperate need as the stallion's, the look irresistibly sucking him in in both cases even though he was still pissed about Leslie's deliberate subterfuge. She might think she had a good reason for it, but as far as he was concerned, no rationalization was good enough for lying to a Dom. He could forgive her that infraction if he could learn the cause for her behavior. Like most dominant men, he was a sucker for a woman with needs, whether they were physical or emotional, it didn't seem to matter.

Strange, he mused, his gaze shifting to the mountains he never tired of looking at, he knew next to nothing about Leslie, and yet couldn't stop thinking about her. No woman had occupied his thoughts to this extent, not even those he'd come to know very well. He couldn't pinpoint what it was about her that made him want to pry every secret out of her. That urge hadn't abated in the weeks following their first encounter, and last night seemed to have whetted his appetite to learn more instead of appeasing it. After she'd left the club, he had pulled Caden aside to glean as much information as he could without asking his friend to breach her privacy. Kurt had no problem doing that himself.

Caden had smirked at his interest and was happy to relate her full name, that she'd been absent from the club for two months without an explanation, and that she wasn't close with any one Dom. Kurt figured she would either stay away from the club for a while to avoid him or ignore him if she returned, so if he wanted answers, his best option was to track her down on her turf. He ruled out showing up at her apartment as she would likely shut the door in his face. That left researching which school she taught at and surprising her where she'd be less inclined to risk attention by arguing with him.

It should give him pause how much he wanted to see her again, how much he longed to know what made her tick, and he craved to sink balls deep inside her snug pussy again. But it didn't. He hadn't felt this rejuvenated in a long time, and the fact it was because of a woman with trouble written all over her didn't faze him in the least. He loved a challenge.

Speaking of challenges. Kurt turned from the corral to see Leland roll out onto the porch by himself, which was an improvement over sitting by his bedroom window. But his focus was still on the family plot instead of on therapy or the ranch. With a sigh, he strode toward the house noticing the cooler air for the first time. Or maybe it was the cold response he expected from his father when he offered to push Leland over to the graves that caused the chill racing over his arms.

Pausing at the steps leading up to the porch, he nudged his hat back and looked up at him as Leland turned to face Kurt. "I see you didn't have any trouble getting out here."

Leland scowled. "It doesn't take much effort to push my skinny frame around."

"You wouldn't be so skinny if you'd eat better and put more effort into your exercises." He held up a hand to ward off the rebuttal he saw forming on Leland's face. "I don't want to argue with you today. If you want, I'll help you over there. Babs picked up the new arrangements yesterday."

"I can feel their loss here the same as I can over there, or anywhere else." Leland swung his gaze back to the small plot. "Do you miss them?"

The abrupt question caught Kurt off guard. His father had never asked him how he felt about his mother or sister's deaths. He'd been too busy grieving after Angela's passing and too intent on blaming Kurt for Brittany's to give his son's heartache a thought.

"Of course I do, Dad. I loved them too." He waited for Leland to say something else, but he just nodded, keeping his face averted, his eyes on the graves, dismissing Kurt yet again. Tugging his Stetson down, he spun on his heel, tossing over his shoulder, "I'm going for a ride."

Kurt ate up the ground between the house and stable with long, frustrated strides, figuring if the stubborn old man could get himself outside he could wheel back in with no problem. He swore the longer he was home the more his father baffled him with uncharacteristic remarks and irritated him with his mulish refusal to put more effort into getting better. The man who had raised him to take pride in working the ranch alongside their employees, no matter how much money they possessed, would never have been content to sit back and wallow in self-pity for this long. He couldn't figure out why Leland seemed to accept he was stuck in that chair for good when his doctors all said otherwise.

"I should've picked up another sub to fuck last night," he muttered as he saddled Atlas. At least relieving his pent-up lust would have settled one of the issues plaguing him today. Unfortunately, once he'd learned Leslie's identity, he'd wanted only her, before and after their scene. The question remaining – what to do about it now?

"WHOA. I was about to ask if you wanted to go for a drink, but I see you already have plans."

Frowning at Amanda, who taught third grade, Leslie followed her co-worker's gaze across the school parking lot and almost dropped her satchel when she saw Kurt leaning casually against the front of her car. She'd stayed at school later than usual to watch the faculty volleyball game, determined to get out of her self-imposed, unsociable rut and find other ways to entertain herself besides going to The Barn. Eying his tall, lean frame and relaxed pose, she went hot all over, her betraying body leaping on board with seeing him again even as her head was telling her *no, stay away*.

"Who is he and where have you been keeping him?" Amanda wanted to know, the appreciation in her eyes revealing the same thing Leslie remembered thinking when she'd first set eyes on him.

With his arms crossed, emphasizing his thick biceps and corded forearms, tight jeans molding to bulging quad muscles and black Stetson tipped low so the eyes were drawn to his rugged, sun-kissed jaw, was it any wonder both she and Amanda had stopped in their tracks as soon as they'd exited the building? But more important than her body's quick spin into overdrive upon seeing him waiting for her was, what was he doing here?

"He's…" What? A friend? Lover? Neither applied to them. "Someone I recently met, and I have no idea what he's doing here. Mind if I take a raincheck on that drink?"

"Not as long as you promise details." With a teasing grin,

Amanda waved and veered toward her car as Leslie took slow, measured steps across the lot, willing her heart to quit racing and her happy girly parts to settle down. The wind blew her calf-length skirt around her legs and whipped her hair into her face. She wore a long-sleeved knit top, but still shivered as a chill invaded her body the closer she got to the first man to leave her still shaken hours after leaving her bed.

Sucking in a deep breath, Leslie clutched her satchel to her chest as she reached her car, and Master Kurt. "How did you know where I work?" was all she could think to ask as he straightened and those coal black eyes tracked over her face.

"It wasn't hard once Caden gave me your last name. You're cold." Reaching behind him, Kurt opened the driver's side door and placed a firm hand on her lower back. "Get in. The wind kicked up in the last hour, making the temperature drop."

Turning, she pressed a hand on his chest, felt the heat and muscle through his shirt, and shivered again, this time for a completely different reason. "Why are you here?" Over his shoulder, she spotted Alan coming out of the school with another teacher, his look curious as he stiffened. Swearing under her breath, she hissed, "You need to leave. I can't afford for anyone here to start gossip about me or to get wind of my membership at The Barn."

"Well, I'm not going to tell them about the club," he replied with a bite in his tone.

Rolling her eyes, she reminded him, "I may not have known who you were that first night, but I've heard how well-connected your family is since. Please, just go. I know I wasn't honest Saturday night and you're probably pissed, but I'm not discussing anything here."

Shaking his head, he pressed her shoulder to nudge her down behind the wheel and then placed himself between the door and the seat, blocking the wind. "Nor would I ask you to, and I'm not mad," he replied, leaning down and surprising her with his answer. "But I am curious about what drove you to ask me to come home with you when you didn't have a clue who I was, and why you kept your real identity a secret the other night. Have dinner with me, and we'll talk."

Leslie wasn't sure she heard him right but breathed easier as she noticed Alan driving off. The two times they were together there had been nothing but sex between them, and he wanted to have dinner? The small part of her she'd tried desperately to keep tucked away thrilled to the invitation, and the interested look in his eyes, and she didn't welcome that reaction. Once she'd developed a reputation as a submissive only interested in the physical appeasement of her needs, the Doms at the club had refrained from pushing for more. She'd suppressed the desire for a relationship for a reason, and she only had to recall her neighbor's pale, pain-filled face when he'd been shot at her front door to remember why.

"Look, I'm sorry I lied. I value my privacy. I appreciate the invitation, but it isn't necessary. As you can see, I'm fine, no traumatic aftereffects from our scene."

Cocking his head, he regarded her for one long, expression-examining moment that set her on edge before answering, "I wouldn't have let you leave the club if I didn't believe you were good to go. I'm offering you dinner, and a chance to get to know each other better, to make it more comfortable the next time we're at the club together. Besides, accepting is the least you can do after trying to pull the wool over my eyes. According to Caden, you're experienced enough to know why you should never lie to a Master."

Guilt, that annoying emotion that wouldn't let her be, reared its head again. Or, maybe the cramp in her abdomen was a continuation of the culpability she'd been experiencing since hearing about Jason Glascott's death and Jake's dire condition. That discomfort went along with the first thread of worry about possible repercussions for her deliberate deception.

"You're thinking too hard, sweetheart, and making too much out of this. Come on, follow me to Rowdy's Steakhouse. It won't be crowded this early on a Monday."

She wanted to, and that's what bothered Leslie – she *really* wanted to, more so after hearing him call her sweetheart in that slow drawl that curled her toes and made her forget about possible consequences for her dishonesty. Because she hadn't been able to forget him in the weeks between their two encounters, she'd be lying to herself if she denied being as curious about him as he seemed to be about her. She didn't want to forgo going to the club again, and having a platonic dinner with Kurt would ease the way for when they saw each other again in the sex-charged atmosphere of The Barn. Given his appeal, it would test her skills at maintaining an emotional distance, but watching several other teachers exit the school, a few casting speculative glances her way, pushed her into accepting without further thought. "Fine. I'll meet you there."

"Excellent. In case you change your mind after I leave, remember, I know where you live." Following that veiled threat, Kurt shut the car door and strode to his truck without a backward glance.

Resisting the childish urge to stick her tongue out at his broad-shouldered back, Leslie started the car and drove behind him all the way to the restaurant. She'd dined at the popular, casual steakhouse a few times and liked the food, but as they parked, her stomach churned with queasy unease over her ability to keep secrets from a Master. None of the Doms she'd played with before Kurt had probed to know anything beyond her physical needs. Not that they were inattentive, but because they respected the boundaries she'd thrown up. This Master didn't seem to care for the dividing line she'd drawn, and given his tenacity in tracking her down, wasn't one to be satisfied with evasive answers. If she couldn't forget him as a stranger who shared her bed one night, what made her think she could keep him at bay now?

Kurt approached her with a crooked smile tilting the corners of his sexy lips and a knowing glint in his eyes. "You're doing it again," he drawled as he took her elbow and steered her toward the doors.

Leslie couldn't deny she liked his firm grip that helped settle her nerves, and the rough scratch of his palm against her softer, smoother skin. "Doing what?" she managed to ask around the distraction as he held the door open.

"Thinking too hard. Relax, It's just a friendly meal between two acquaintances."

She tilted her head in question as she looked up at him. "Is that what we are? Acquaintances?"

"For now."

That smooth, confident reply set the butterflies to fluttering in her abdomen again. She tried pulling from his hold, but he only tightened it on her elbow as he spoke to the young hostess who eyed him as if she'd like to have Kurt for dinner. Leslie couldn't blame the girl as they followed her twitching butt across the peanut-shelled wood-planked floor to a corner table. But she could, and should control the frisson of jealousy that irritated her to no end. If he was interested in the immature, flirty type, that was all the better for her.

"Thank you." Kurt nodded at the hostess and pulled out a chair for Leslie. Bending, he whispered in her ear, "I prefer a woman with blue eyes who hides secrets to the open ogling of a kid."

This time Leslie succeeded in removing her arm from his grasp as she shook her head and sat down. "Do you have eyes in the back of your head?"

"No, just good peripheral vision and experience with reticent subs."

"Look." Leslie leaned forward as Kurt took the seat opposite her. "I've never needed to spill my life's story to play at the club, and don't intend to start now. Teaching is everything to me, and I won't let you jeopardize my job by insisting on getting personal, so if that's what you're…"

"Stop." The cold whiplash of his quiet voice halted her tirade and sent a shiver down her rigid spine. "That's the second time you've suggested I would, in any way, risk your job by revealing the nature of our relationship, and I don't appreciate it. Do not do so again."

Oh, wow. For the first time ever, Leslie was tempted to revert to her submissive side outside of the club by saying, "Yes, Sir," and apologizing for her unintentional accusation. From the moment she'd first stepped foot in The Barn, scared and excited about exploring the lifestyle she'd been fascinated with for years, she'd found it easy to set aside her independence long enough to embrace submissive needs that were new to her. But never when away from that sexually-charged venue.

Not trusting her voice, she nodded and took a sip of water, waiting for him to elaborate on what he wanted from her. Obviously, he didn't mind making her stew while they ordered before sitting back and giving her one of those dark, intent looks that stirred up her juices while putting her on high alert.

"I'm not asking for much, Leslie. Just an explanation for your attempted deceit Saturday night. If I wanted to berate you or delve into every aspect of your life, I would have stuck around following the night I took you home from the bar. I won't lie and say I'm not interested in learning more about you, because I am. But we have time. Tonight, I'll settle for an explanation for lying to a Dom." A teasing glint softened his gaze. "It's not as if I'll mete out a punishment here."

Leslie blushed and shifted as tingles raced across her buttocks at the mention of 'punishment'. The sudden longing to pull down her panties and drape herself over his hard thighs unnerved her as much as the craving to surrender to the sweet seduction of blissful pain wrought from this man's, this Dom's hand.

Kurt's jaw went taut as he leaned forward again. "Keep looking like that and we'll be heading out to the parking lot for a quick reprimand."

Jerking back, she pulled her head out of the clouds as the waitress delivered their drinks and a basket of homemade rolls that made her stomach growl. Trying to defuse the tension, she reached for a roll and buttered it as she replied, "I admit I suspected you recognized me Saturday night, but a lot of our previous encounter after we got to my place remains a blur." She shrugged. "How was I to know what was real or imagined? I don't recall either of us revealing anything except our first names, but like I said, my memory of that night is sketchy. I figured it was easier to play it safe and pretend we'd never met. That was a mistake, and I apologize, again."

There was more to it than that, but Kurt let it slide. She'd agreed to dinner and sat across from him with a flush on her face, her blue eyes wary but still holding a hint of interest and arousal. He could work with that until he got her to open up more. Why he was so determined to pull out every secret she harbored, he hadn't a clue. Maybe taking on the challenge of getting to know her would be a good distraction from second guessing his father all day, or maybe it was just an intense case of lust and dominant annoyance over failing to breach the wall she'd built around her private emotions. The only time he'd failed at anything had been in keeping his sister from self-destructing, and that was a painful lesson he did not want to repeat.

"Good enough." He took a swig of beer before delighting in shocking her by suggesting bluntly, "You can atone for your mistake by agreeing to a short affair, one that includes getting together both at the club and outside it." Her hand jerked, sloshing her drink before she set the glass down, the surprise on her face priceless, her puckered nipples poking against her top unmistakably telling.

"Are you blackmailing me?"

The tremor in her voice bothered him as much as her misconception and he snapped in reaction, "Of course not. I wouldn't do that." He paused to suck in a deep, calming breath before continuing. "You intrigue me, Leslie, I won't lie. Do I want to delve into your deepest, darkest secrets? You bet your ass, I do. Would I resort to underhanded tactics to do so? Fuck no. Barring that, I want you. One night of fucking you isn't enough and one scene at The Barn doesn't cut it. If you can *honestly* tell me you don't want more of what I have to offer, say so and we'll go our separate ways tonight and pick someone else to play with at the club."

"That simple?" Her expression said, 'no way'.

Leslie's skeptical look and tone amused him. Was she not used to straight forward talk and ultimatums or just leery of him? "It is for me." That wasn't altogether true. He wouldn't find it easy to walk away from her, but he'd do it if she insisted.

The waitress delivered their food and Leslie stalled from answering Kurt by sampling a few bites of the fiesta chicken first. He could tell the moment she came to a decision. Her tense shoulders relaxed and she lifted her eyes to reveal a spark of excitement that outweighed the uncertainty she still possessed. It was the reason for that uncertainty he hoped to eventually root out.

"Okay, I'll see you outside the club, as well as there, as long as we're careful so no one can connect us to The Barn. Keeping that part of my life secret hasn't been easy since my co-workers are the only people I see daily and occasionally socialize with."

"Is the reason for not expanding friendships something else you don't want to share?" he prodded.

She pondered her answer for a moment, looking away before facing him again. "Yes, since the reason is the same for not being able to enter into anything serious with you, or anyone else. Please, let it go at that."

"In that case, no more than a month ought to be enough for both of us to get what we want out of a limited relationship. How's your chicken?"

Both his time limit and quick topic change caught her off guard, and that worked for him. Keeping her second guessing her own motives and whether what he proposed would be enough for her should work in his favor eventually. At least, that's what he was hoping for.

Chapter 7

L eslie started second guessing her decision as soon as Kurt insisted on following her home after dinner. Glancing at his truck in her rearview mirror, she wondered what it was about that enticed her into throwing caution to the wind and going against her better instincts to indulge her physical needs. It wasn't as if she couldn't get those cravings met with another Dom. The disappointment she experienced when he added a time limit after she agreed to his proposition didn't make sense. She should have been relieved he wanted nothing more than a brief affair to work out whatever this was between them and then move on.

"I must be out of my mind," she muttered, pulling into her apartment complex. She should have asked him for more details on what he expected from her outside of the club. She'd grown comfortable at The Barn after learning what to expect whenever she went. Maybe not who she might play with or the details of a scene, but with the regular members, the public exposure and the different aspects of BDSM that worked for her. The last time she'd indulged in an affair had been almost five years ago, way before her life had been upended and she'd discovered the pleasures and benefits of alternative sex. She'd gotten more from one-time scenes with men she'd just met at the club than during the months-long vanilla relationships with men she'd gotten to know well. Since there was no point in hoping an affair would lead to something permanent, like she used to, she'd never considered seeing any of the Doms outside of the club.

Leslie slid out of the car, pausing as Kurt parked next to her and opened his door with an expression on his face that sent a familiar wave of heated lust rushing through her veins, the same quick response she felt upon seeing him for the first time at the bar and then again last weekend. She hadn't considered he might want to start this affair tonight, but she thought wrong as he came toward her with a smoldering black-eyed look of purpose. Unsure of herself, and her motives for accepting his proposal, she tried to put him off.

"Thanks for seeing me home. I have to get up early, so…"

"This won't take long," Kurt interrupted, holding out a hand for the keys to her apartment.

"So, we're going to jump into this affair?" She handed him the keys, wincing at his censuring stare. Leslie heard the tartness in her defensive tone as well as he.

"Our affair began as soon as you agreed, but tonight I only have time to mete out your punishment for lying to me." Unlocking the door, he pushed it open and stood aside to let her enter first.

Leslie expected retribution for that infraction, and as she sidled by him and he brushed a hand over her buttocks, a quiver of combined anticipation and dread tiptoed down her spine. She couldn't fathom what Kurt desired from this relationship after their two odd encounters, but that hand swipe spoke volumes on what he wanted tonight. And God help her, she yearned for the painful distraction of his punishing hand with an intensity that shook her and had her floundering as she tossed her satchel onto a chair before facing him inside her apartment again.

A taunting smile curled his mouth as he shut the door and stepped toward her. "What's wrong? You weren't nervous with me at the club, and since I wasn't inebriated the last time I was here with you, I remember clearly how you begged for my attention." Gripping her arm, he tugged her over to the sofa, sat down and pulled her over his lap.

As soon as Leslie's nervously fluttering stomach landed on Master Kurt's muscle-hard thighs and he held her down with a hand braced between her shoulder blades, everything inside her settled. Releasing her stalled breath on a *whoosh*, she braced her hands on the floor as he inched her skirt up over her panty-covered butt. Feeling the need to say something, she looked around with a teasing smile of her own. "Anything I can say or do to change your mind?"

"There's always the safeword, other than that," he shoved her panties down, "no."

"Okay." She put her head back down, thrilling to the cool exposure of her buttocks and the warm caress of his calloused palm despite the vulnerable unease this position always conjured up.

"No pleas or extra apologies?" He squeezed one globe, the tight grip drawing a shudder.

"I learned long ago never to try and dissuade a Master intent on punishment. And I know when I'm in the wrong," she admitted in a muffled reply, goosebumps racing across her backside as he released his hold on her flesh.

"You intrigue me, sweetheart." Kurt swatted her right cheek, hard enough to warm her skin and sting. "You don't hesitate to admit when you're guilty of wrongdoing and don't balk at accepting your punishment." Another smack generated more heat and a deeper pain that snagged her breath. "But anything personal sends you running." Two rapid slaps bounced her cheeks, the ache and burn seeping deeper into Leslie's flesh. "Do you go to the club just to appease your submissive needs?"

Four blistering blows threatened her composure, forced her to tighten her arms to keep from sliding forward and bite her lips to prevent a sob from the throbbing pain encompassing her entire butt. Master Kurt allowed her time to adjust to the discomfort and to answer his question, softly rubbing the abused flesh. Taking a deep breath, she let the pain work in her favor, waited for it to spread down between her legs and warm her pussy. He helped it along by brushing his thumb along her seam, the light stroke enough to draw a damp response.

"Sir?" She shook her hair out of her eyes as she peered up at him and saw his focus on her bare butt and his teasing thumb.

"Answer my question, Leslie," he ordered without looking at her.

"Yes," She huffed, annoyed with his persistence, but not surprised.

"Thank you." Lifting his hand, he added pressure between her shoulders as he braced one leg over her calves and proceeded to spank her in earnest.

Peppering her quaking buttocks with a steady volley of hard swats meant to hurt and redden pulled a tortured sob from Leslie. Responding like always, she slid into a tailspin of emotional turmoil before finding her way to that quiet place where she could float without a care. With the deepening, swelling pain came tears of release, the escalating heat spreading over her cheeks wiped away the ever-present coldness of her lonely life and bleak future. Kurt shifted to land a devastating blow to the under curve of both buttocks before delivering the same to the tops of her thighs. She couldn't move her legs or shoulders, and the struggle to wiggle her hips to ease the pain soon wasn't worth the effort. With a shuddering sigh and tears running down her face, she embraced the pulsating numbness starting to cover her flaming backside as she lay limp as a noodle over his lap.

KURT RELISHED the moment she gave herself over to the hot pain, could tell when she let go of the tension riding her and landed in that zone where nothing else mattered except her Dom's attention. Which she had in spades. His palm ached by the time he tempered the smacks to softer taps before halting to rub the trembling bright red flesh that was hot to the touch. She would have a few bruises come morning, and he liked knowing he marked her, and that she would think of him when she saw them and every time she sat down. He'd been hard on her on purpose, letting her know what he would not tolerate over the next few weeks. He couldn't do anything if she insisted on keeping her secrets, but he wouldn't accept lying or deliberate deceit.

The glistening slit between her legs tempted him, but he'd have to wait a little longer to bury his cock inside that snug, squeezing pussy again. That's part of the sacrifice for keeping her guessing while trying to hurdle the walls she'd erected around herself. Turning her over without pulling up her panties, he held her close as she sniffled into his neck. She wasn't the first woman he'd brought to tears, but somehow, the shaking of her slender frame against him, her soft, trembling sighs and cute, watery hiccups got to him on a level no other sub managed. It had been that way from the moment he rescued her from a street thug and looked into her sad blue eyes.

Kurt placed two fingers under Leslie's chin and nudged her head up, the look in her drenched eyes sucker-punching him in the gut. She might still appear uncertain of him and his motives but at least she wasn't pulling away.

"Are you with me, sweetheart?" Releasing her chin, he trailed his hand down her arched neck, over one plump breast and up her smooth thigh until he reached the soft flesh of her bare labia.

"Yes." She shifted against his cupped palm with a low, needy moan. "Sir?"

"*Mmmm*, I think you still don't deserve to be let off the hook for your lie." He rotated his wrist until her seeping juices coated his palm, unable to hold back a grin when she narrowed those glazed eyes as he wiped the dampness on her thigh. Before he changed his mind, he lifted her off his lap and pushed to his feet. "I've got to get back to the ranch and check in on my dad. I'll call in a few days." Hauling her against him, he took her mouth in a slow, searing kiss before walking out without a backward look.

Leslie stood there glaring daggers at Kurt's retreating back until he closed the door behind him, her whole body vibrating with unfulfilled arousal, her buttocks hot and throbbing. And yet, for all her frustration, she hadn't felt this good in a long time. It still amazed her how a long, hard spanking worked to soothe her rioting emotions. She might still be uncertain about entering into an affair, but not about with whom.

By the time she climbed into bed, wincing before she rolled onto her stomach and took the pressure off her sore butt, she was looking forward to seeing Master Kurt again. With the punishment for her lie out of the way, she figured he would be as ready as she to fuck again next time they got together.

She figured wrong.

KURT JUMPED BACK from the mustang's rearing front legs, swearing under his breath at the close call his inattention brought about. Yanking back the lassoed rope that missed the irritated stallion's neck for the second time, he leaned against the rail and gave the agitated horse time to calm down before trying again. Endeavoring to gain the wild mustang's trust might prove as fruitless as attempting to get inside Leslie's head. And if he couldn't quit thinking about her long enough to focus his full concentration on the potentially dangerous task he'd set out for himself then he was in big trouble.

Running a hand behind his sweaty neck, he eyed the now still horse who gazed at him from across the corral, his eyes wary, his dilapidated body quivering from his exertions. Damned if that mistrust didn't remind him of Leslie. He'd finally succeeded in getting the stallion to take a carrot from his hand that morning, which had prompted him to try catching him for lead training. It was hard not to compare that short-lived success with talking Leslie into an affair, and then admitting he had a long way to go. Usually, he was a patient man, he'd had to be in dealing with his father the past ten years. But seeing the neglect the mustang had suffered tested the patience he needed to restore his health and teach him all people weren't bad. With Leslie, the moment he'd seen the desperate loneliness in her blue eyes when he'd escorted her home that first night, he'd been drawn to discover the source and erase it for her.

"I am so fucked," Kurt grumbled, pushing away from the fence. Refusing to give up for the day, he moved slowly toward the mustang, keeping the rope at his side. If there was a way to get through to the animal, he would find it, just as he would come up with something to breach the walls of one stubborn submissive.

With a toss of his head, the stallion trotted along the fence as Kurt neared, obviously still disinclined to allow him to loop the rope around his neck. Determined to give it one more try, Kurt lifted the rope, braced his feet apart, twirled the lasso above his head and waited until the wild horse stomped close enough to let the noose fly. He didn't know who was startled more by his success, him or the horse. Gripping the rope with both gloved hands, he tightened his stance and arms against the mustang's surprised, angry reaction of rearing up.

Several cowhands, including Roy, quietly took up guard along the fence as the two of them danced around the enclosure in a battle of wills. Dust flared up as Kurt struggled to stay clear of flailing hooves while maintaining his hold against the strong jerks of the stallion's head. He might be three hundred pounds under-weight but that didn't mean he wasn't still a force to be reckoned with given his size.

By the time he managed to calm the mustang enough to stop his agitated rearing, Kurt's arms ached and his heavy breathing matched the horse's labored huffs. "That's a boy," he crooned, approaching the quivering equine with slow steps. "There, all done. See, no harm done." With a cautious hand, Kurt slipped the rope off and stepped back as he took off with a loud neigh.

"You're fucking crazy, you do know that, don't you?"

Kurt pivoted at the sound of Caden's amused voice, a grin wreathing his dust-smudged face as he spotted his friend and Connor leaning on the rail next to Roy. "I've been told that a lot since bringing that son-of-a-bitch home. What brings you two out here?" Jumping the fence, he joined them on the other side.

"I didn't get a chance to tell you they were stopping by to pick a Thoroughbred for a gift," Roy said. "I decided to wait to see if you survived that stunt before wasting my breath."

"Ha, ha. Thanks for having my back, even if you doubted my persuasive skills." He cocked his head as he eyed the brothers. "A gift? It must be for Sydney since I know Tamara wouldn't trade her Arabian for anything else, but don't you have a few to pick from?"

"You're right, she wouldn't. We did have one, but by the time Caden talked Sydney into trying a new mount, we'd already accepted a good offer on her. Your inventory has more to pick from right now." Connor looked at the mustang and shook his head, his jaw tightening with a flash of anger swirling in his blue eyes. "Do you know who's responsible?"

"No, which is why I'm not in jail for assault, or worse," Kurt replied.

"Sydney talked me into buying a pathetic excuse for horse-flesh last year and babied that animal back to health. Gotta admit it was worth the time and effort she put into the animal." Caden jerked a thumb toward the mustang. "If you're half as successful with him, you'll have a good horse."

"I think so too," Kurt agreed. "Come on, I have a few mares between eighteen months and two I think would be a good fit for your wife."

The perfect opportunity to work on getting Leslie to open up fell into Kurt's lap as he led Caden and Connor to the stables housing the Thoroughbreds for sale. Opening the door, the scent of fresh hay and horses greeted them, as did the soft whin-nies from some of the equines sticking their long, sleek necks over the half gates to their stalls. He stopped at the few he thought Sydney would love, the ones with spirit but easy to control.

"Belle here is my favorite." Kurt stopped at the stall of a dark chestnut mare with a white star blazoned on her forehead. She butted his arm looking for a treat, which Caden provided by opening his hand with a sugar cube.

"She's a beauty." Caden stroked a hand down her neck, eying her size with a frown. "Taller than I was looking for though. With Syd being pregnant, she'll need to be more careful when riding."

Connor snorted. "Good luck with that."

"How about if I hold her until after the baby comes and give her to you as a baby gift," Kurt offered, not surprised by the caution Caden exhibited with Sydney. The redhead was an enticing trouble magnet whose soft spot for animals amused him and drove her husband nuts when she extended it toward the ranch animals.

"That's too generous. I'll split the cost with you and we'll both give Belle to her."

Connor smirked at his brother. "In the meantime, good luck

dissuading her from coming home with the worst the auction house has to offer tomorrow."

Seeing the frustrated resignation on Caden's face gave Kurt an idea. "How about if Leslie and I come along? If they're busy chatting, maybe Sydney won't pay as much attention to the auction ring."

"That might help," Caden returned as he entered the stall to get a closer look at the mare. Running a hand down her withers, he looked over his shoulder with a small grin. "You and Leslie outside of the club?"

Kurt shrugged, ignoring Connor's amused look. "We're giving it a try. She thinks it's just for sex."

"It's not?" Connor asked, surprised. "I never pictured her interested in anything beyond a few scenes at the club."

"I don't think she is, and I'm still trying to decide if I am." He looked at Caden. "Anyway, I could use Sydney's help, if you think she'd be willing."

Resting his hand on Belle's flank, Caden tipped his hat back and drawled, "Willing to help encourage a relationship between a friend and a Dom? You'd be hard-pressed to stop her."

"Excellent. We can seal both deals over lunch. Babs made friend chicken."

LESLIE'S PHONE beeped with a text message, a welcome distraction from Alan, who insisted on joining her for lunch in the teachers' lounge. Her pulse jumped at seeing Kurt's name, not a good reaction for someone who needed to keep an emotional distance. "Excuse me, I should answer this."

Turning away from Alan's frown, she read Kurt's message, her interest piqued despite wondering why he wanted her to go out with him on what sounded like a double date. Once she'd agreed to an affair, she assumed that meant getting together at her place for a night once in a while, a few hours that might or might not include having dinner together. She never imagined he would want to go out as a couple with others, or take her to a ranching auction. With agriculture listed among Montana's top industries, she'd lived in the state long enough to learn how popular auctions for livestock were, she just never thought of attending one for fun.

Curious about his motives, she texted back a simple *Why?* His honest, straightforward answer rattled her.

Because going out together is what couples who are having an affair do.

Unable to resist, she typed back, *I thought this was about sex.*

You thought wrong. I'll be at your place by 4:00. We'll go to dinner after the auction.

He clicked off and she looked up to see Alan's curious stare. "Everything okay?" he asked.

"Yes, sorry about that. A friend wanting to meet up tomorrow after school."

Reaching for her bottled water, her hand jerked when he wanted to know, "The same friend I saw you with in the parking lot the other day?"

Leslie refused to lie, and maybe telling Alan she was seeing someone would keep him from asking her out again. "Yes. We met about two months ago." She kept the circumstances of her and Kurt's initial introduction and the weeks since to herself.

"That's good." He smiled but hinted for more. "He looked familiar."

The door to the lounge opened and two more faculty members entered carrying their lunches. Ignoring Alan's last statement, Leslie gathered up her trash and stood to greet them. "Here, Mike. You can have my seat. I'm finished and need to get back to my classroom. Alan, thanks for joining me. Catch you later."

Regardless of her misgivings about entering into this affair and worrying about the potential heartache of getting too close to anyone, Leslie returned home the next day looking forward to the evening out. And when she opened her door to Kurt and a warm fuzzy surrounded her chest to go along with the now familiar surge of heated blood flow through her veins, she was able to stave off the instant panic for now.

"Hi. I'm glad I guessed right and stuck with jeans." Dressed in his usual denim and cowboy boots, today he wore a dove gray, button down western shirt with the long sleeves rolled back to just below his elbows, enough to draw the eyes to the corded muscles of his forearms.

Those midnight eyes shone with an appreciative light as he looked her over. "You look as good in jeans as you did dressed as Cleopatra, sweetheart. Ready?"

Leslie was powerless to resist his extended hand or the warmth in his gaze. "Why aren't you cold?" she asked with envy, shivering against the much cooler evening breeze as they walked to his truck.

Grasping her waist, Kurt lifted her onto the passenger seat. "I'm warm-blooded, more so when you look at me like that. Keep it up and you'll find out how fast I can strip those tight jeans off you."

"Threats like that only make me want to try harder to get you to act on them, and I'm not the one who planned a night out," she reminded him. He'd refrained from fucking her the last two times they were together. She wasn't naïve enough to believe he hadn't been with other subs during the five weeks between the first and second time they'd met, but she couldn't understand why he was holding back now, or why it bothered her so much.

Kurt waited until he slid behind the wheel, started the truck and looked at her askance as he backed out before answering, "Is this aversion to socializing something I need to address? If so, tell me now so I can add it to your other issues we need to work on."

Huffing in annoyance, she snapped, "I don't have issues. Just because I'm not a social butterfly doesn't mean there's something wrong with me."

"Oh, make no mistake, you have issues. But we'll deal with those in good time. Try and enjoy yourself. Auctions can be fun, even if you're not bidding."

They were crowded, loud and smelly. Okay, and fun, Leslie admitted thirty minutes later. Seated on a hard bleacher between Sydney and Kurt, with Caden on Sydney's other side, she looked down into the pen in front of the auctioneer's booth and smiled at the pair of miniature horses up for bid.

"Oh, wow, they are so cute." She sighed and leaned forward, her heart breaking for their poor condition.

"The dogs would love to romp with them. They're the perfect size…"

Caden interrupted Sydney with an emphatic shake of his head. "No. Absolutely not. My working dogs don't need playmates, and we don't need two more rescues."

"I guess you'll have to get them, Leslie. Do you have any pets?" Sydney turned inquisitive green eyes on her.

"No, not since I was a kid and we took in a stray mutt. Cute little thing." She remembered naming the small dog Mitzi and how she used to curl up in bed with her.

Sydney elbowed her with a sly grin. "I'm sure Kurt can find room to board the ponies at his ranch. From what I hear, that place is huge."

"No," she shot back before Kurt could say anything. "I can't afford them and know nothing about horses." And the last thing she needed was to become indebted to him for caring for her pets, even if those two little ponies were adorable and in sad need of attention.

"I could teach you, and I have plenty of room. Let me know if you change your mind," he said around the piece of straw he was chewing on.

Why she found that sexy, Leslie had no idea. Maybe the ache

for his full possession occupying her mind was responsible for finding everything he did sexy, and arousing.

Bidding signs started going up and like with each new showing, Leslie and Sydney tuned out the auctioneer's rapid-fire chanting, choosing to talk between them instead. As soon as the miniature horses were sold and led out, Sydney sighed in disappointment.

"If you loved me, you would have bought them for me."

"I do love you and no, I wouldn't. You've amassed enough extra mouths for us to feed," Caden returned dryly before gazing over at Leslie. "You have to forgive her. She was an only child and used to getting her way."

He winked, the light in his eyes teasing. Before she could reply, Sydney defended herself. "Being an only child had its benefits, but it would have been nice to have a sibling to hang out with. How about you, Les? Any sisters or brothers?"

"One sister." Leslie paused, wincing at her mistake and the stab of pain that always pierced her heart whenever she thought of Roslyn. Her limited conversations with people at the club had never included personal chit chat and the question caught her off guard enough she answered honestly instead of relating the details of the fictional past given to her in the program. "We're not close and haven't spoken in years." God, it hurt to say that. Tears pricked her eyes and she started to rise, to excuse herself and find a restroom, but Kurt grabbed her hand and squeezed. That simple touch, the hard pressure of his larger grip, calmed her enough to get herself under control.

Sydney distracted her further by saying, "You'll have to come out to the ranch soon. I'll get Tamara to join us for a ride, maybe a picnic while it's still decent weather."

"Thanks, but I don't ride." Not to mention that would be getting too close to people she refused to grow attached to or, God forbid, end up putting at risk if Edwin Glascott ever succeeded in unearthing her whereabouts. She didn't need

Detective Reynold's telling her the death of one of his beloved sons in prison had bolstered his determination to come after her. Regardless of his ability to hide his involvement, she would never forget or underestimate the hatred he'd spewed toward her in the courtroom.

"Really? You've been here longer than me, haven't you?"

Leslie shrugged and turned her eyes on the cattle being ushered into the bidding pen. "Over three years, but I'm with second graders all day, not horses."

Sighing, Sydney shook her head. "Oh, girlfriend, we have got to get you out more."

She let that comment slide; there was no use arguing when she couldn't give a reason for the argument. They went to dinner at a small Italian restaurant and while she enjoyed the evening out, and the food, the reminders of everything missing in her life kept her edgy, especially when talk turned toward Sydney's pregnancy.

"I was hoping to make a trip back home before winter," Sydney said after they'd given their orders to the waitress and she had passed on alcohol. "I'm due in March and after another long winter, I'll be ready to take up drinking again." She turned to Caden. "Will you have time to make a trip to St. Louis for Thanksgiving, if the weather holds?"

He reached over and squeezed her hand, an indulgent look softening his face. "I'll make time," he replied before turning a probing gaze on Leslie. "Do you get the chance to visit home much, Leslie?"

Once again, the unexpected personal question jolted Leslie. Since she'd kept to herself so much since relocating to Billings, she lacked practice in getting comfortable with her fake past and her mind still automatically conjured up her life in Reno. As she struggled to get her thoughts in order, suspicion began to form a tight knot in her belly. That made one too many pokes into her private life for her comfort.

"No, I don't. There's nothing there for me anymore." Pushing back from the table, she stood as she fought against the mistrust entering her head. "Excuse me, I need to find the restroom." She spun around and wound her way through the tables toward the lit-up bathroom sign before they said anything. She placed the blame for the subterfuge solely on Kurt, admitting it didn't surprise and irritate her. From their first encounter he'd shown too much interest in her beyond the sex for her peace of mind, and she was well aware there were Doms who insisted on seeing to sub's emotional needs as well as their physical. That's why she'd stayed clear of them after just one scene or two.

Master Kurt left her no choice but to back off from this relationship, but before she did, she craved one more night with him, yearned to wrap her arms around his larger, harder body one more time and experience the mind-numbing pleasure of his thick cock pummeling her depths again. Just a few more hours to relish the contentment of being taken over completely before she turned away the only man she couldn't forget.

Kurt stood as she returned to the table, his eyes sharpening as she sat down. "Problem, sweetheart?"

Schooling her features, she forced a confident smile as she saw their food arriving. "No, I'm fine."

He nodded and the conversation remained on neutral topics as they ate, but Leslie still thought it best to end this after tonight. Sitting next to him in the truck, her body hummed in anticipation of submitting to him one more time. But just like the two times they'd gotten together this week, he pulled her in for a kiss that fired her up on all cylinders and then walked away without giving her what she wanted most. Himself. He left her aching after a long, thorough, panty-dampening lip-lock and a promise to call the next day.

Standing inside her open door with her damp thong clinging to her skin, pining for his touch, she glared at his swaggering retreat, refusing to call him back and beg. He paused after opening the truck door and looked back at her with a taunting grin that made her grit her teeth in frustration. "I'll call you. Behave, Leslie."

"Maybe I won't answer," she muttered as he settled behind the wheel, her disappointment a palpable throb deep inside her. She didn't see his satisfied grin as he drove away.

Kurt drove back to the ranch happy with the progress he'd made tonight with Sydney's help. His girl liked animals but had only owned one pet. She wasn't an only child, as he assumed, and he didn't believe her when she said she and her sister weren't close. The reason for that evasion remained to be solved. After living in Montana for several years, she still hadn't sat a horse. That could be rectified easy enough if he could get her out to the ranch.

All in all, this affair had been going his way nicely until she returned from the restroom and remained aloof during dinner, her eyes revealing the wariness he thought they had gotten past. She likely didn't understand why he was putting off fucking her again, and planned on remedying that problem tomorrow night at the club. His plan to show her he was interested in exploring more than the physical side of a Dom/sub relationship would have to wait so he could appease her mind about the depth of his desire for her. His only concern was once he did, she would start pulling back, and he wasn't ready to let her go yet.

Chapter 8

Reno, Nevada

Edwin Glascott ignored the softly uttered condolences as people he didn't give a shit about filed by him in the cemetery. Standing over his youngest son's grave was a place he'd never imagined he would find himself. His boys had been his legacy and everything to him, and there had been and still was nothing he wouldn't do for them. Now, he would leave one burial to plan for another, having gotten the call that morning informing him of Jake's death. Hadn't he warned them off the drugs? When they'd ignored him and ended up offing that pathetic store owner, hadn't he cautioned them to lay low and give him time to get them out of that mess?

He'd never loved anyone until he'd laid eyes on his infant sons. Their bitch of a mother walked out when Jason turned two and Edwin hadn't cared. In fact, he remembered watching her drive away with a sense of relief and gladness it would be just the three of them from then on. Money, as he'd discovered after earning his first million, had its uses and opened doors that would otherwise have remained closed. His boys had gone to the best schools, wore designer clothing, drove top of the line cars. So what if they got into scrapes now and then? They were young, just sowing a few wild oats, nothing he hadn't done in his youth except shooting someone. After he learned about the witness, his livid temper with the entire fucked-up situation nearly exploded, and his rage only intensified when she refused to be cowed by his threats. When threats didn't work, his hired thug botched the attempt to silence her and then she disappeared, driving his fury to new heights.

As he watched his son's casket lowering into the ground, white-hot fury burned inside him, a smoldering rage unlike anything he'd ever experienced. He could think of nothing except revenge, wouldn't accept any other outcome but the death of the woman responsible for his sons' fate.

Spinning away from the grave, Edwin stomped toward the limo. There was one more funeral to get through, and then, by God, he would enact his revenge.

———

I'LL BE a little late tonight, but I'll meet you at the club.

Leslie read Kurt's text as she entered her apartment the next day after school. She wasn't going to stay away from the club just to avoid him, even though it was tempting to hide out at home for a few weeks until he got over this idea of an affair. No, she needed to move on, go back to playing the field at The Barn and that, more than anything else would get her over this infatuation. She should have considered that during the weeks she'd stayed home, unable to forget the stranger who had come to her rescue one night in more ways than one.

I'll be there.

The simple reply didn't commit her to spend the evening with Master Kurt and she left it at that as she got ready. Rifling through her closet, Leslie wished she owned some fetish clothing like Nan always wore. She'd never wanted to dress to catch as much attention as possible like she did now. There were enough Doms to go around and she wasn't picky, at least she never had been before. But as she reached for a silky, thigh-skimming sheath, she found herself considering Master Kurt's hot gaze as he stripped it off her instead of any of the other Doms still free of a commitment.

Bemoaning her idiocy, she tossed the dress onto the bed and took a quick shower. By the time she fixed a light dinner, dressed and made the thirty-minute drive to the secluded club, it was close to nine o'clock and she breathed a sigh of relief when she didn't see Kurt's truck in the parking lot. Walking inside, she stowed her shoes and hung up her light coat, eager to hook up with someone before Kurt arrived. Once he saw she had moved on to another Dom, he should be happy to let go of the whole idea of an affair.

So why did her palms grow clammy and her heart slam against her chest as she entered the playroom and scanned the crowd? Forcing a mental head shake and adjustment, she spotted Avery and Nan seated at the bar and padded over to join them. At least Sydney wasn't around to say anything about her and Kurt. That was a plus. Avery waved her over with a welcoming smile and patted the empty stool next to her.

Leslie hopped on the seat, returning her smile. "Hi. What are you drinking?" She nodded toward the half-filled glasses in front of them.

"A new white wine they just got in. Here, try a taste, you'll like it." Avery handed Leslie her glass

"Oh, you're right," she agreed, taking a sip as Master Grayson strolled over from behind the bar.

"One more?" he asked, shifting the toothpick stuck in the corner of his mouth that reminded Leslie of Kurt chewing on a blade of straw during the auction. Grayson and Kurt shared the same sun-darkened, rugged complexions and wore their black hair long enough to brush their collars, their eyes often holding the same piercing gazes when they looked at a sub even though Grayson's were a striking gray/green compared to Kurt's velvet black.

Leslie smiled. "Yes, Sir. Thank you." Too bad Grayson had fallen so hard for Avery two years ago when she'd first moved to Willow Springs and went to work at the diner. Leslie wouldn't mind letting him put her through her paces again as he had the one time he'd invited her to play.

"Oh, yum, incoming pussy magnet," Nan whispered after Grayson handed Leslie her wine and strode down the bar out of earshot. "Man, if only I wasn't so fucking crazy about Master Dan." She fingered the ornate collar around her neck as Avery and Leslie followed her stare to watch Master Mitchell stop to visit with Masters Greg and Devin and the petite blonde seated between them.

Standing an inch or two over the tallest members put the doctor's height around six foot four, his lean build deceiving as the tight T- shirt stretched across his broad shoulders and snugly around the thick muscles of his upper arms could attest to. In his early forties, his salt and pepper hair and matching goatee added to his appeal and accounted for the good doctor's popularity among the subs. Leslie caught sight of him last week but hadn't met him. The two ex-FBI now dude ranch owners who weren't here last weekend appeared enamored of the new sub they shared, if Leslie guessed correctly from their fond, protective gazes.

"Have you met Master Mitchell, Leslie?" Avery asked. "Or Kelsey, Greg and Devin's new girl?"

"No, but I agree with Nan." She shifted on the barstool, having decided the new Dom was the diversion she needed from thinking about Master Kurt and didn't argue when Nan waved him over.

"Ladies, what can I do for you?" Mitchell's eyes swung

toward Leslie holding a gleam of interest. "I don't think we've met. I'm Master Mitchell."

Leslie took his hand, praying he didn't notice the slight tremor of her palm against his. She wasn't sure if the sudden attack of nerves came from the intruding image of Master Kurt's face in her head or pleasure from this Dom's attention. "I'm Leslie. Nice to meet you, Sir."

Cocking his head toward Nan and Avery, he smiled and drawled, "Please tell me you're not spoken for like these two."

"No, I'm not." The sense of betrayal tightening her throat didn't sit well with Leslie and she shoved it aside as Master Mitchell squeezed her hand.

"Then I'd welcome the opportunity to get to know you better upstairs."

Neither she nor Kurt had asked for monogamy and since Leslie didn't intend to continue with their short-lived affair, all was fair, right? So why did a sharp prick of guilt cut her to the quick as she replied, "I'd like that, Sir."

He didn't give her time to second guess her decision, tugging her off the stool and asking for her limits and safewords as they wound their way upstairs and over to the St. Andrew's Cross. His hands were gentle as he stripped the dress off and trailed his fingers down her legs as he removed her panties. Her heart pounded against her chest as he turned her to face the apparatus, not because he was binding her arms above her head to the wide upper X, but because she wasn't getting that warm rush she enjoyed with Master Kurt. God, had he already ruined her for other Doms?

KURT REACHED the loft and spotted Leslie bound on the St. Andrew's Cross right away. As he eyed her slim, bare back, spread legs and white, soft ass, he didn't know who to be pissed at the most, her or his dad. He shouldn't have let Leland goad him into an argument right before he'd left. If the stubborn coot didn't want to go to therapy or work at getting back on his feet, Kurt ought to leave him alone to stew in the misery of his own making. The problem was, he cared too much to do that, just as his strong feelings for Leslie wouldn't allow him to give up on her regardless of her continued obstinance. Maybe, if those glimpses of a desperate, lonely ache reflected on her face weren't continuing to wreak havoc with his conscience, starting with the first time she'd looked up at him, he would find it easy to wash his hands of her and walk away.

Between wanting to solve the mystery of her solitary life and the driving lust to fuck her in every way possible, he wasn't about to let this little rebellion deter him from his goals. Mitchell flicked him a questioning look as he approached, checking the tightness of the ankle cuffs before rising to greet him.

"Kurt. I hope your scowl isn't because of something I've done."

"No, in fact I'd like to thank you for preparing my sub for me." Leslie's muscles tightened under Kurt's hand as he caressed her clenching buttocks.

Mitchell's eyes darkened, his gaze cutting toward Leslie. Fisting a hand in her long hair, he pulled, lifting her head. "Is this true, you're with Master Kurt?"

She bit her lip, both men noticing the guilt swirling in her eyes as she looked from one to the other before her trembling mouth went taut and she replied with a thread of defiance coloring her tone. "We never agreed to be exclusive."

Kurt winged one brow upward and crossed his arms over his chest. "I don't share. In case I neglected to mention that, now you know."

Moving back, a hint of amusement crept into Mitchell's expression. "I'll step aside and let you two work this out. Leslie, look me up if you decide to ditch Master Kurt again."

Kurt waited until Mitchell walked away before leaning against Leslie's back, loosely circling her neck with his hands and whispering in her ear, "Don't you think you should have told me before you accepted another Dom's invitation?"

"I didn't think it would matter."

A slight tremor ran through her body as he tightened his hands on her throat, just enough to remind her of his control, and what she'd agreed to. "Once again, you thought wrong, and you're not being completely honest. You'd rather back away than risk revealing more about yourself, like you did last night."

She tried to turn her head to look at him then released her breath in a huff when his hold wouldn't allow it. Her throat worked under his hands as she swallowed and said, "You have no right to pry."

Now it was his turn to sigh with exasperation because, damn it, she was right. Stepping back, he ran his hands over her shoulders, down her arched back and palmed her buttocks. "You're right about that, but not about how you let me know you weren't happy with me." Digging his fingers into the soft globes, his thumbs slipped between the fleshy mounds to tease the sensitive area. "I'm disappointed you would resort to such a tactic instead of talking to me. Five swats with my belt or say red and we're done. What will it be?"

Leslie couldn't think straight, not with Master Kurt's hands on her, the displeasure in his deep voice filling her with guilt and regret. She'd been a fool. What made her believe she could simply walk away from him now when she couldn't forget him after one night together? Now she found herself torn between her ever-growing need for one man and her determination to ensure no one else would come to harm because of their association with her.

She heard the slide of his belt as he removed it and quaked inside. Goosebumps popped up across her backside as he trailed the supple leather over her flesh. To this day she didn't under-

120

stand how an aching, hot butt could calm her rioting emotions while drawing tears of discomfort, or how the hurt could eventually morph into pleasure. But there was no denying her body sang in tune to the silent threat, warmed to the promise of blissful pain and the pleasure induced forgetfulness it could lead to. If he allowed it.

Kurt reached around and cupped one breast before pinching her nipple. "Give me your answer, Leslie."

Need won out over good intentions and she succumbed to the pull of that deep, commanding tone. For the first time in almost four years, she didn't want to think in terms of 'what if', instead, opting for 'why not'. "I'll take the swats, Sir."

"Excellent." The soothing caress of his hand over her clenching cheeks warmed her as much as the approval in his voice. "Count them for me."

Leslie faced ahead as Master Kurt took a step to the side and swung the belt. With a snap, the thick leather licked across both buttocks, leaving a prickling burn in its wake. "One, Sir." She bit her lip and braced for the second strike, which landed below the first with sharper intensity. Sucking in a breath, she whispered, "Two, Sir."

Pausing, he coasted a hand up and down her back. His silence and the delay unnerved her until the throbbing ache dulled enough to rouse her yearning for more. Her cuffed hands and ankles kept her arms and legs bound but her hips were free to lift and push back in silent entreaty.

"That's my girl," Kurt crooned, dropping his hand and delivering another blistering stroke.

Searing pain encompassed her butt, drawing a gasp before she could respond, "Three, Sir."

Clenching her hands, Leslie bore down to accept the last two which came fast and hard, as she guessed they would. Tears fell down her face even as she embraced the pulsating agony. Her head went fuzzy, that pleasant euphoria that took her away from the unpleasant sensations until they slowly changed into needy arousal.

Before her senses cleared, Master Kurt released the restraints and turned her around to bind her again with her back to the cross. Leslie moaned as he cupped her mound and leaned forward, his dark face filling her vision, the roughness of his clothes reminding her of her complete nakedness. Lowering his coal-black head, he bit one turgid nipple and pressed hard against her swollen pussy. She'd never craved anyone as much as she did him, never wanted to be fucked as much as she longed for the burning stretch of his cock pounding into her. God help her, she didn't know what she would do if he backed away from her again.

"Tell me, Leslie," he whispered against her lips, "why did you think I would be okay with you turning to another Dom?"

Looking into the black depths of his intent gaze, she knew she couldn't get away with anything except the stark truth. "Because you only want to get into my mind now, unlike that first night when we met."

"Is that so? You think you know me, do you?"

The silky undertone of displeasure in his voice caused her a second of unease, and then he pressed his middle finger inside her pussy and nothing else mattered as she thrust against his palm with an aching plea. "*Please.*"

Kurt shoved aside his annoyance with Leslie, acknowledging she had a case for jumping to the wrong conclusion about why he hadn't fucked her again since their surprise reunion. Eventually they would discuss that insecurity as well as anything else she was keeping from him. But not now, not tonight.

With his eyes on hers, he moved back enough so she could watch him free his cock with one hand while continuing to swirl his finger inside her slick pussy with the other. "I love how you're always wet, sweetheart, always ready for more, whatever it is I want to do to you and with you." A shudder went through her damp body as she eyed his hard, hot flesh springing into his hand. "Like that, do you?" He squeezed his shaft while stroking her puffy clit.

"Yes, I do. Sir." Her pelvis jutted forward, a gush of cream coating his finger with her quiet moan.

"Then I think it's time I proved how wrong your assumption of me is." Pulling out of her clasping channel, he swiped his wet finger over her smooth labia, transferring the dampness as he sheathed his cock.

Reaching behind her, Kurt grasped Leslie's ass, holding her hips still as he speared her flesh in one thrust. "Eyes down," he ordered, working his way back out of her tight pussy until only his cockhead remained nestled inside. "I want you to see how much I want you." He rammed straight up inside her again. "I want you to learn what a restraint it has been for me to hold back, to go slow for your benefit regardless of my own lust."

Leslie shook her head, her tawny hair sliding around her tense shoulders, her blue eyes wide with both surprise and arousal. "How was I supposed…" She gasped as he leaned forward and drew a nipple into his mouth, suckling the hard tip as he pumped inside her clutching pussy. *"Oh, God."*

Kurt worried her nipple with his teeth before releasing the pink bud to give her a stern look. "You were supposed to trust your Dom. Watch."

Her gaze swept down as he pulled her pelvis forward for easier use of her pussy. He eyed their joined bodies along with her, loved the way her tight inner muscles clamped around his pummeling shaft, the soft grip of her puffy labia enfolding his steely girth and the warm gush of her juices easing his way.

Their breathing grew labored along with his forays in and out of her clutching body. Her breasts, coated with a damp sheen, jiggled with each pounding thrust, her tight, pinpointed nipples begging for his mouth again. His lust for her turned into a greedy conflagration, clawing at his balls with a voracious need that grew with each ramming stroke, hardening his cock into an aching demand.

Panting, Leslie shook in the restraints, straining toward him, her eyes remaining glued to his pummeling dick. The look on her face undid Kurt, the edgy arousal that changed to a need so strong she winced as if in pain. Her womb clenched and flooded with liquid heat as she clamped around him and screamed in pleasure, the spasming grips of her climax pulling his orgasm from his balls to spew into the latex and orbit him to the same plane of ecstasy she appeared lost in.

"Still think I don't want you?" Kurt rasped as he dragged his cock slowly out of her still clinging depths, his breathing as heavy as hers, his heart still thundering in his ears.

Leslie's flushed face turned even redder. "I…" She inhaled, struggling to catch her breath, and when she did, a wicked gleam entered her eyes. "I may need a few more examples, Sir. You know, just to be sure."

His lips twitched. She didn't reveal her lighthearted side often enough. "I'll see what I can do about that." He squeezed her warm ass, her grimace drawing his smile. "I wouldn't want you to make the same mistake twice." Releasing her bonds, she fell against him with a laugh and he held her soft, naked body close, wondering how long she would cling to him before pulling away again.

OVER THE NEXT TWO WEEKS, Leslie's resolve to guard her feelings was put to the test as Master Kurt left her with no doubts about whether he desired her or not. He instructed her to get dressed up and took her out to dinner at the most expensive restaurant in Billings and then for a drive outside of town to fuck her on the hood of his truck, leaving her hard-pressed to concentrate on her students the next day.

They returned to her apartment after going out for hamburgers and miniature golf and he fucked her against the wall as soon as they got inside, ripping her panties off in his haste. She'd fallen into bed still vibrating from the three orgasms and his tender look as he'd told her good-night.

He attached nipple huggers and inserted dual bullet vibrators before taking her to the newest comedy film. Seated in a private balcony booth, he cut off her laughter more than once with a flick of the switch that started the toys pulsating in soft waves inside her pussy and rectum but refused to let her climax until on the way home. She'd stumbled into her apartment on wobbly legs, still chuckling from the movie.

Damn, that had been the longest two hours of her life, Leslie mused with a fond smile as she tried grading papers. But that hadn't been as bad as missing him the following day when he called but they didn't go out or last night, when he'd lifted his face from her needy, saturated pussy, his mouth glistening with her juices, two fingers still moving inside her and asked what made her decide to move to Montana. The personal question had caught her by surprise and stalled her climax, angering her. She winced as she remembered snapping at him, telling him it was none of his business and how he retaliated by slamming out of her apartment. She'd feared that would be the end of their affair and then fretted over the tight constriction around her heart the thought caused. But he called thirty minutes later, just as she'd crawled teary-eyed into bed, and made plans for the next evening as if nothing had happened, and she'd fallen into sleep without further thought or stress.

Leslie leaned back from the desk and stretched with a rueful shake of her head. He thrilled her, confused her and pissed her off, but she was having fun for the first time in four years. Not just getting her submissive needs met, which was what she'd been settling for since joining The Barn, but actively enjoying herself with a man for the first time in a long, long while. The only nagging question that kept intruding and marring her enjoyment was, *How long can this last?*

Reno, Nevada

"I'm in."

"It's about fucking time," Edwin snapped back, impatience tightening his gut as he gripped the phone. Swiveling his office chair around to look out the window of his downtown high rise, he cursed the time it had taken to find someone with the skills he needed and then make sure that person was willing and trust-worthy to hack into government data. In the weeks since he'd buried his sons, the itch to see the woman responsible for their deaths wiped from the face of the earth had intensified. It wasn't right she got to live after she'd sent his boys to that Godawful place where they didn't belong.

"Look, I told you this wouldn't be easy. The best hackers in the world work for the government so I had to move slowly and carefully."

"It didn't take you long to jump at the amount I offered," Edwin snapped back, his impatience a live wire zapping his control. "Now, give me the information and we can be done." He wrote down the whereabouts of the state's witness, made arrangements for the final payment to be sent and then contacted the hired mercenary waiting to carry out his next orders. Once his man took care of Leanne Davis, a.k.a. Leslie Collins, Edwin might hire him to do away with the hacker. He'd learned early in his business dealings never to leave loose ends lying around for others to pick up.

Fifteen minutes later, satisfied with the mercenary's promise to act fast, Edwin poured himself a whiskey and silently toasted the soon-to-be demise of the person who caused him such insurmountable grief.

Two days later

Leslie checked the time, grabbed her purse and started out to her car with a warm rush of anticipation threatening her resolve to stay detached from relationships. Somehow, during the last two weeks of going out with Kurt followed by submitting to whatever demands he commanded of her body, the need to guard against involvement had been overtaken by the escalating desire for more of Master Kurt's sexual dominance and Kurt, the wealthy cattleman's attention. It wasn't until her phone rang as she slid behind the wheel and she saw Agent Summers name on the display that she was reminded how life could change on a dime.

It was too early for Cathy's monthly check-in, which meant something had happened. Leslie's throat closed as she gripped the phone, a sense of foreboding overshadowing her excitement for spending the day at Kurt's ranch.

"Cathy. What's up?"

"I'm sorry, Leslie. Word has just come down our system has been hacked. We're not sure when, but best guess from our IT department is at least forty-eight hours. There's no way to know if your identity has been compromised but we can get you moved within hours."

Moved? Start over again with yet another name in yet another city where I know no one? Where I'll be alone again? No, she couldn't do it, *wouldn't* do it. She remembered how the girls from the club reached out to her a few weeks ago despite the way she'd held back from getting too friendly and her eyes went damp; the faces of her second graders who were catching on to reading and learning addition and subtraction, of the ones who still needed extra help and the spontaneous hugs from others popped up, and her stomach cramped.

She thought of Kurt and her chest constricted. This was what she got for letting herself hope she could have a life here, for dropping her guard and getting involved, for losing the battle of caring too much.

"What are the odds Glascott is still holding a grudge or that whoever hacked your data bases would pass on the information?" She was grasping at straws, but didn't care.

"This isn't a Reno casino game were playing, Leslie. I didn't want to add to your burden by saying anything sooner, but we've kept feelers out on Edwin Glascott and rumor has it he took those boys' deaths hard and has been in a volatile state of mind ever since. Do you honestly want to take the risk of staying where you're at, because I can't force you to leave?" Cathy's exasperation and empathy rang in Leslie's ear.

She didn't want to cause her grief. She also couldn't bear it if, by staying, she put someone else in the crosshairs of whoever Glascott might send after her. God help her, if it was just herself she had to worry about, she would honestly consider saying to hell with the risk. But the last attempt on her life proved how easy someone else could get caught in the crosshairs and end up hurt, or worse, for no other reason than they were with her.

"I can't be ready in a few hours. I have to contact the school principal. I won't disappear on them without a word." And she longed to see Kurt one more time, owed it to him to tell him good-bye in person. The tears swimming in her eyes dripped down her face and she swiped them off with the back of a hand. Lamenting her circumstances wouldn't help, only delay the inevitable.

"I'll get everything set up. Call me when you're ready. We'll take care of the apartment. We can also take care of contacting your boss, if you'd rather," Cathy offered in understanding.

"No, but thank you. It's Sunday, but he won't mind if I call him. I'll make up a family emergency and be in touch this evening."

Leslie hung up before she changed her mind. Those fleeting thoughts of staying and taking her chances were dismissed as soon as the memory of her neighbor jerking and falling against her from a drive by gunshot wound popped up unbidden. Her fingers shook as she started the car and pulled out, her mind racing with what she would say to Kurt. He was astute at reading her expressions and seeing through her lies. The truth might be her best bet, after all, what could he say or argue about? He'd likely escort her off his ranch as soon as she told him everything he'd been pestering her to reveal about herself, and she wouldn't blame him.

As she left Billings and got onto the highway, following Kurt's detailed instructions, she railed against being thrust into another situation where doing the right thing required such heartache. With despair clogging her throat and cramping her abdomen and her thoughts centered on what she would tell him, Leslie didn't notice the car on her tail, or see it swerve around until it sped by her so fast she jumped.

"Moron," she muttered, glaring at the taillights disappearing over the rise ahead. There was little traffic on this outstretch, with nothing but miles of prairie on either side of the road with an occasional turnoff here and there. The isolation made it easy to let her mind wander until a loud rapport, sounding like a car backfiring, came out of nowhere, disturbing the peaceful quietness of the countryside. Startled, Leslie gripped the steering wheel tighter, her rear tire blowing in the next instant, shaking her even more.

With a panicked cry, she hit the brakes as the car lurched to the side, icy fear twisting around her heart and stealing her breath as another shot pinged against the back side. Leslie barely had time to acknowledge someone was shooting at her before she hit a rut and went airborne for one horrifying second. A terrified scream ripped from her throat as the car came crashing down on the passenger side, tossing her against the door with a jarring, painful impact, her head cracking on the window before leaving her dangling sideways in the seatbelt. Her vision swam, bile rising into her throat. Pain engulfed her whole body, dread cramped her muscles and then agonizing despair pulled her under.

Chapter 9

"I talked to your therapist last night." Kurt glared at his father and then glanced at the time again. Leslie was late, which put him in no mood for another sparring match with Leland. But, after speaking with Tamara last night at the club and hearing how much more he was capable of doing with a little effort, Kurt felt this couldn't wait. "Give me one good reason why you can't put yourself out to go to physical therapy more than once a week."

Leland's jaw went taut and he shifted his stormy eyes out the window again. "It's my life. Quit nagging me about it."

Frustrated, Kurt strode across the bedroom to stand in front of Leland's chair and bent down to grip the armrests, getting in his face. This attitude of his was so unlike the strong-willed parent who never let anything hold him back. As he'd often told Kurt, ranching was in his blood and there was nothing he would rather do, regardless of the wealth that afforded him a much easier life.

"Tamara said you should be strong enough by now to move from the parallel bars to a walker, and eventually a cane, but you refuse to try. Damn it, Dad, you're the one who should be running this place, not me, not yet."

Leland's shoulders went rigid. "I'm seventy-two and ready to take it easy. You just want to continue shirking your responsibilities Get out of my face."

Tires crunched on the gravel drive out front, drawing Kurt's expectant gaze out the window. Disappointment swamped him as he saw it wasn't Leslie but one of the hands. He thought they'd been getting along great the past few weeks, and he had no complaints. He enjoyed taking her out as much as he'd relished her willing submission to anything he proposed afterward, and she appeared equally pleased with their budding relationship. If she didn't show up soon, he would go after her. He wasn't ready to let her go yet, not without a fight. But, first things first.

"I returned to help you as soon as I could, so I don't know how you can accuse me of shirking my duties." It was time to lay what was really standing between them out on the table. "You're the one who drove me away when you refused to admit Brittany's death was no one's fault but her own." Leland's face paled, a bleak expression entering his eyes, but he still stared out the window. Kurt sighed, wishing he could get through to him. "I came home because I only want what's best for you, and I know damn good and well you don't want to sit around inside this house feeling sorry for yourself. Even after Mom and Brittany's deaths, you refused to turn over the running of things to either me or Roy. Be very careful you don't let your stubbornness drive me away again."

Turning his back on him with that idle threat, Kurt missed the spasm of fright crossing Leland's face and the sheen of sorrow in his father's dark eyes. Stomping down the hall, he shoved Leland's uncharacteristic, annoying behavior to the back burner and engaged fully on one stubborn submissive. Detouring into the kitchen, he put the fried chicken he picked up from Dale's Diner into the refrigerator. He'd been looking forward to taking Leslie for her first ride today, nestled in front of him on Atlas, snacking on chicken as he showed her his ranch. Since she was over an hour late, they might not have time to ride as far as he'd planned, and if he couldn't get her out here, there wouldn't be time to ride at all.

Snatching his hat off the hook by the front door, he stepped outside, the brisk October air cooling his temper as he walked to his truck. Maybe she had a good excuse, he considered, driving down the long lane toward the highway. Or maybe her sense of direction was as piss-poor as Sydney's. That possibility worried him. He hated to think of Leslie this far out of the city, surrounded by the endless miles of wide-open spaces and worrying about finding her way to his place.

Once on the highway, he drove toward Billings, hoping to see her on the way. The flashing lights of emergency vehicles forcing him to slow down after a few miles filled him with sudden dread. Sweat pooled at the base of his spine as an icy knot of foreboding gripped his abdomen. Idling down to a stop, he saw the under carriage of a car lying on its side out in the field to his right, several cars and trucks pulled over along the side of the road, Grayson's official sheriff's cruiser and the county ambulance. It wasn't until he hopped out that he got a clear view of who was sitting up on the gurney, her face white as a sheet, a bandage on her forehead and eyes glazed with shock and pain.

A fear-induced adrenaline rush propelled Kurt forward, his pulse skyrocketing into his throat with anxious apprehension. He caught sight of Grayson walking around Leslie's upended vehicle with a deputy, the scowl on his face sending another wave of uneasiness through him. Balling his hands into fists, he paused to suck in a deep, fortifying breath before taking the last few strides to reach Leslie's side.

"I'm sorry, you'll need to stay back..."

Kurt whipped his cold-eyed stare on the hapless EMT, shutting him up. "She's with me," was all he said. Nodding, the medic stepped back to give him room to stand by Leslie's side. Leaning over, he brushed his lips around the bandage covering her bruised, swollen forehead. "Jesus, sweetheart, tell me you're all right."

Kurt's dark face swam in front of Leslie's vision, the deep, concerned rumble of his voice reaching inside her to dispel the last remnants of fog clouding her head, keeping her insulated from the pain and terror of what just happened. She'd roused to voices calling to her, careful hands freeing her from the seatbelt, more hands catching her as she tumbled down and then gently extricating her from the wrecked car. A cold chill snaked down her spine as she recalled the rapport of gunfire and the loss of control, and shuddered in lingering fear of realizing someone had come after her on purpose.

Glascott, if it was him behind this attack, had wasted no time following the breach of sealed, government files. She doubted he would execute his own dirty work. No, he'd likely hired it out, and that person could very well still be aiming at her from the trees. The field where her car had gone careening off the road might be a vast expanse of prairie grasses, but a mile or two off the highway on the other side lay tree-shrouded woods that made for excellent cover.

She didn't realize she'd turned her head toward those woods until Kurt placed two fingers under her chin and nudged her to face him again. "Leslie, baby, talk to me. Are you okay?" When she nodded, her throat too dry with fear to talk, he looked at the EMT who had shifted to her other side. "Can you tell me her condition?"

"Concussion, bruised ribs from the seatbelt, left arm is swelling and should be x-rayed but she's refusing to go to the hospital. She kept mumbling something about it not being safe, but that was likely from being disoriented."

"Or, it could be because she knows something we don't,"

Grayson stated, joining them with his sharp, assessing gray/green eyes zeroing in on Leslie.

Shit. Hiding her emotions from one narrow-eyed, astute Dom was difficult enough. Now she had two of them regarding her with intense concern.

"What's that supposed to mean?" Kurt demanded to know.

"It means your girl didn't just have an accident. There's a bullet lodged in her front tire and one embedded too damn close to the gas tank to make this anything except a deliberate attempt on her life." The fury in Grayson's tone matched Kurt's darkening, thundercloud expression.

Now what do I say? With her head and arm throbbing and the three faces staring at her turning blurry, Leslie closed her eyes and leaned her head back, unable to cope with anything right now except to reiterate no hospital. "I thought those sounded like gunshots, which is only one reason why I'm not going to the hospital." Her voice emerged from her constricted throat as a reedy whisper but she opened her eyes to see they heard her just fine.

"You're in no condition to make that decision," Kurt snapped.

Grayson took charge by asking the medic, "Do you know where the Willow Springs clinic is, one street over from the town square?"

The young man nodded. "Yep. We can take her there as long as there is a doctor waiting."

Catching on, Kurt whipped out his cell. "There will be. I'll follow you."

Leslie watched Kurt and Grayson turn away and heard Mitchell's name before Kurt started conversing with the new doctor. If she weren't so scared, and didn't hurt so much, she might have gotten excited about the prospect of the hot doctor putting his hands on her. But as the EMT slid the gurney into the ambulance and then hopped in to join her with a rap on the side

BJ WANE

to get them going, all she could think about was the jeopardy she was putting everyone in.

THE NEXT TWO hours were the longest of Kurt's life. Mitchell hadn't hesitated to open the clinic on a Sunday afternoon, but friendship came second to his patient as soon as Leslie was wheeled into the exam room where the weekend nurse waited with him. After his friend shut the door in his face, he'd turned to find Grayson leaning against the wall, arms crossed, toothpick returned to his mouth, regarding him with a solemn expression.

"I need to know what you know," he said.

"Yeah, well I need to know a hell of a lot more than that." Unable to stand still, Kurt paced the hall, the quietness of the clinic grating on his nerves as much as the sheriff's silent, watchful gaze. Frustrated, worried and scared to the bone, he finally whirled to face his friend and ground out, "She has a sister, haven't a clue where or even what her name is. Her apartment is devoid of any personal articles and her life was lacking in personal involvement until I pressed her into an affair. Oh, and she likes animals but hasn't owned a pet since she was a kid. There, does that help?"

"Now that you've got that out, why don't we put our heads together and figure out who would want to harm her, or worse," Grayson drawled.

Kurt went rigid with rage imagining someone deliberately setting out to kill Leslie, vowing right then and there not to let her out of his sight until the fucker went down. "Jesus, Monroe, I haven't a fucking clue." He sliced a hand through the air between them, swearing. "She's a second-grade teacher, for God's sake."

"With a secret past no one knows anything about, an aloof manner when it comes to forming relationships or friendships

136

and, according to you, she doesn't even have a photo of her sister in her apartment. Want to know what I deduce from all of that?"

Put all together like that, Kurt could come up with only one possible answer, one that sent a frisson of unease slithering under his skin. "Witness protection?"

Grayson shrugged. "I could be wrong."

"But you, we could be right, and it does explain a lot." And added layers to his worry. "If they hear of this…"

"They'll move her."

"No one's moving her anywhere for a while," Mitchell said, stepping out of the exam room. "I caught the last bit of your conversation, and from Leslie's expression, so did she. She has a concussion, which we knew. Her arm isn't broken but badly banged up, as is her left hip and thigh. All in all, she's damn lucky that's it, but she needs rest."

"Then I suggest the two of you help me convince her to come to my place while the Feds get this figured out. She'll be safe there. I've got over fifty cowhands who are excellent shots and between the sensors along the fencing and hidden cameras everywhere, Grayson, you know how secure our property is."

"Decision's hers, but I'm willing to go to bat for you. Hell, we didn't like partying anywhere on your land as teens because your security was too fucking good. I imagine it's even better now."

"Damn straight." Kurt turned to Mitchell. "Can I go in now?"

"Be my guest. I don't envy you the battle you're in for."

NOW I HAVE THREE STERN-FACED, determined Doms to contend with. Leslie shivered as she looked at the men entering the small room, their chiseled faces etched with stone-cold determination, their eyes showing varying shades of warm concern mingling with banked fury on her behalf. She could have staved off Kurt's pushy insistence for answers if need be, but all three of them? She was doomed to reveal everything, and she knew it before a word was said. Grateful the nurse had already stepped out after helping her dress, her wobbly legs forced her to sit back down on the exam table.

"What?" she asked, stalling. Sheriff Grayson was as good at his job as sheriff as he was as a Master at The Barn. The pain shot Dr. Hoffstetter administered had already kicked in, but the woozy numbness it wrought wasn't enough to deflect the forceful impact of those looks.

Kurt moved to her side and ran a hand down the back of her head and hair, the soothing caress tempting her to lean against him. But that would strip away the last of her defenses, so she forced herself to stay upright and worked up a teasing grin. "Sorry, looks like I'll be late getting to your place."

His hand tightened in her hair, his knuckles pressing against her nape, the grip holding her head immobile. "Not funny, Leslie. Why would someone deliberately shoot at you?"

She sighed, her shoulders slumping. "Cutting right to the chase, aren't you?"

"Do we have time not to?" Grayson growled.

Leslie succumbed to the inevitable. "No. I have to make a phone call and then," her voice caught and she yanked her head hard enough for Kurt to drop his hand, "I have to leave. I'm sorry I brought this down on you." Her gaze swept the three of them, but her words were for Kurt.

Mitchell continued to lean against the wall, staying silent but eyeing her with both medical concern and dominant frustration. Grayson crossed his arms and continued to glare, both of them leaving it up to Kurt to address that statement.

His eyes flashed with temper but his response, a blunt, emphatic, "No," warmed her even as it got her ire up. Before she could vent, he surprised her by saying, "Call your liaison in Witness Protection and tell them you have a safe place to stay with me. Or better yet, let me talk to them. I have a few words to tell them about their ability to keep you safe."

"How did you know?" The relief over having the secret out couldn't prevent a cold slither of fear for him, and anyone else who came near her. If Glascott had sent someone after her, he wouldn't get paid until he'd completed the job.

"It didn't take long to figure it out once I found the bullets in your car." Grayson took the few steps to her other side. "I can vouch for the security surrounding the Wilcox ranch which includes how many cowhands all proficient with a rifle?" He glanced toward Kurt.

"Fifty, at last count." His black eyes bored into her. "They not only spend their days riding our property, they have to carry rifles and know how to shoot fast and accurately to keep our live-stock safe from predators. A bear or cougar attack can spring without warning. Someone *might* be savvy enough to disable a sensor or avoid a camera, but alarms will signal such a breach, in the bunkhouse, main house and offices." His voice turned gruff as he held out his hand. "Come home with me, sweet-heart. We can discuss your plight further when you're feeling better."

Mitchell spoke for the first time since re-entering the room with Kurt and Grayson. "You shouldn't make any important decisions for the next twenty-four hours, and not while you're heavily sedated, like you are now."

Leslie knew when she was beat, only unlike four years ago when she'd railed and despaired over having to enter the program and forge a new life, this time, God help her, she was going to risk holding onto what she had for a little longer.

Ignoring the presence of Mitchell and Grayson, she gave Kurt her full attention, and her stipulation. "Fine, I'll come to your place, but I'm not sleeping with you." If the sheriff's office and whatever help Grayson got from the Feds couldn't stop this threat, and fast, she needed to prepare for leaving everything, and everyone she cared about again. She couldn't do that if she and Kurt continued to grow closer.

Grayson snorted and walked out. Mitchell raised a sardonic brow before leaving them alone. Kurt was blunt and to the point. "Sweetheart, there's never been any sleeping when we've been together. Let's go."

He was going to be difficult, Leslie knew it. That didn't bother her, which meant she was already in deeper than she should be, or wanted to be.

KURT SWALLOWED his irritation over Leslie's terms, not surprised she would try to pull back from their relationship. She'd agreed to his protection, and for now, that was enough. On the drive back to the ranch, he listened as she called the principal and arranged for an emergency leave of absence and then insisted she put it on speaker when she pressed the number for her Witness Protection contact. They indulged in a bit of a pissing contest, but he and Agent Summers came to a grudging agreement when Leslie spoke up with another provision, tacking on a two-week limit to her stay. By the time he drove through the gates onto his land, he could tell by her set face she wouldn't budge on that.

"How far back does your property extend?" she asked as he pulled in front of the house.

"Farther than you can see. Don't worry," he added, seeing the look of consternation crossing her face. "I stand by what I said and told Agent Summers. You're safe here, I'll see to it." Leaning across the seat, he cupped her nape and drew her forward for a deep, possessive kiss.

He nipped her lower lip before shifting back, his cock jerking as she licked over the bite with a narrowed eyed glare despite the definite pucker of her nipples under the blue knit top. "I told you, I'm not…" She clammed up as soon as he held up his hand, an immediate submissive response that he wasn't above exploiting.

"As you can see, we're not in position to sleep. Wait there and I'll help you inside."

Of course, she didn't, opting to display her annoyance by sliding off the high seat of the truck. He got there just in time to catch her as her legs gave out, either due to pain or her drug-induced grogginess.

"You better get over this stubborn streak or another part of your anatomy will be smarting as much as your side and head." The warning had the desired effect – she didn't complain as he swung her up into his arms and carried her inside.

Leslie cast an uneasy glance around the large foyer and into the den. "I'm fine now. You can put me down."

"Relax. No one is here today except my father, and he's ensconced in his room at the other end of the house." Kurt released her legs and let her stand but kept an arm around her waist.

"Is he doing any better?"

Her thoughtful concern after her ordeal helped ease his tension. If she could think of others so soon after such a trau-matic event, she wouldn't let herself crumble under another upheaval of her life. She'd shown the same considerate solicitude when he'd first told her about Leland in the hopes she would share more about herself. Now that she was here, he would have more opportunities to coax her out of her shell.

"He could be back in the saddle by now but refuses to put out the effort to get there. I don't understand his attitude," he admitted, leading her toward the hall. "He seems content to get by with the bare minimum of therapy and let Cory, his aide, or me help him otherwise. I'll introduce you when you're up to meeting him, just remember not to take any flak from him. You'll be comfortable in here and there's an attached bath." He ushered her into the blue bedroom, glad she wasn't the type of woman to gush over the obvious signs of wealth exhibited by the size of their home and property. Having suffered a trauma that landed her in Witness Protection, he imagined she'd learned what was of real value in life a long time ago.

Leslie turned to him all of a sudden, that familiar look of desolation and desperation clouding her eyes as she uttered in a fretful whisper, "Kurt, Sir, are you sure? I couldn't bear it if someone on your ranch came to harm because of me."

Her slip in addressing him as a sub revealed the effort it was taking for her to agree to stay here. One of those tight, uncomfortable sensations in his chest grabbed hold. The unaccustomed pangs started in the last week and the one now was the strongest yet. "You concentrate on recovering and let me worry about the safety of everyone here. That's an order." She opened her mouth then snapped it shut with a nod. "Good girl," Kurt murmured, running a hand down her back before giving her ass a friendly pat. "Mitchell said for you to rest. I'll check on you every hour this afternoon. In the meantime, think about what you want me to get from your apartment. Or I could take you into Willow Springs to pick up a few things. I'm sure word of what happened has already spread."

She lifted a trembling hand to brush her hair back. "I'll worry about all that tomorrow as long as you have a spare toothbrush and I can borrow something to sleep in."

"Yes to both. Lie down, Leslie."

Leslie waited until Kurt walked out, closing the door behind him, not needing the authoritative tone and command to give in to the stress and drug-induced weariness to stretch out on the double bed with a shaky sigh. A swath of sunlight streaming through the wall-dominating window splashed across her butt, the warmth adding to the little tingles from that light, friendly tap. If he continued with small, innocent touches like that, she was doomed from the get-go reverting their relationship into a platonic one.

Over the next few hours she heard him come in several times, felt him sit next to her and run his hand down her back and over her butt as she mumbled vague answers to his probing questions. By the time she blinked open her eyes all the way, an amber glow illuminated the background of the mountain view outside the window. Spotting the glass of water and pain pills on the nightstand, she downed two and then lay there a moment wondering what insanity had prompted her to risk everything by agreeing to stay here. And then she thought of leaving, starting over in a strange place, getting used to a new name and a new existence, and a slow burn of anger coiled through her aching body.

Fuck Edwin Glascott and his two murderous sons, she swore, rolling off the bed. She'd trusted Kurt when he'd been a stranger and again when she'd met Master Kurt. It didn't surprise her she trusted the wealthy landowner with resources she couldn't imagine to keep her safe. Padding over to the window, she took in the stables and barns across several acres beyond the landscaped lawn around the house. Even though it was Sunday, she could make out several ranch hands riding in the fields among a large herd of black cattle and noted the rifles either held across their laps or nestled in scabbards at their sides. Even those employees working around the outbuildings wore guns tucked into the back of their waistbands, and Leslie realized how seriously Kurt had taken the threat against her, and how fast he had moved to inform his employees.

The thought of something happening to him, or anyone else, added to her rage against the Glascotts even as it sent her pulse into a rapid, erratic beat of panic. Praying for a swift and final end to this threat, she turned from the window and padded into the bathroom. The royal blue towels and decorative tile in varying shades of blue that drew her eyes longingly toward the shower matched the soft, comfortable bedspread she'd rested on.

After a quick face and hand wash, she debated whether to hunt down Kurt and get something to eat or crawl back into bed. The loud rumble of her stomach as she left the bathroom settled the matter and she went in search of her host.

Instead of finding Kurt when Leslie reached the center of the house and took in the spacious great room, dining area and kitchen, an older man turned his wheelchair away from the bay of floor to ceiling windows to give her a cool, appraising once-over from eyes as coal-black as Kurt's. He masked the bleak expression on his face as he'd gazed out the windows, his look turning sharp and angry. Tensing her shoulders, she braced for Kurt's father to lay into her for bringing trouble to his son and ranch.

"You're the one my son has been spending so much time with lately. He has enough to do without adding your problems to his responsibilities."

Leslie regarded him coolly for a moment, deciding the best way to deal with a recalcitrant old man was the same as she would a confrontational second grader. Head on. Fisting her hands on her hips, she blinked back the encroaching wooziness from the pain meds before stating in a firm but polite tone, "Kurt doesn't need you to run interference on his life for him. From what I've heard, all he needs from you is a little effort on your part to improve your condition."

She almost laughed at the comical shock on his face, but then her heart rolled over as a look of hopeless despair entered his eyes as he swiveled his gaze toward a photo sitting on the fireplace mantle. Leslie didn't need him to tell her the pretty young woman with coal black hair and striking blue eyes was his daughter, the sister Kurt mentioned who had died tragically in a car accident at the age of twenty. What did it say about her that she knew so much more about him than he did her and yet he never hesitated to offer his protection?

Leland's gruff voice pulled her from regrets she couldn't do anything about. "Kurt is outside but you shouldn't wander out of the house without him by your side."

Since she didn't know what to say in the face of his sadness she offered an olive branch of friendship. "I'm sorry if having me here has disrupted your life. I'm sure you know your son is a difficult man to argue with when he's hell bent on something."

"Yes, I know." He spun around to face the stunning mountain view. "I also know you must mean a great deal to him. He only gets so overprotective and demanding with those he cares about the most. Go help yourself in the kitchen and then sit down before you fall down."

He sounded as commanding as Kurt just then and since she didn't want to risk collapsing either, she left him to his brooding to mull over what he'd said and wonder about the guilt etched on his face. The thought of Master Kurt having deeper feelings for her besides that of a Dom gave her a thrill of pleasure even as it ratcheted up her anxiety over this new threat to her peace of mind that could force her to start over far away from him and Montana. That small burst of happiness confirmed she'd made the right decision to end the physical side of their relationship now in preparation for the worst.

Chapter 10

Kurt had wasted no time in sending out an employee text as soon as he'd settled Leslie, explaining the situation and offering paid leave to anyone who was uncomfortable with the risk of having her on the ranch. It didn't surprise him no one took him up on the offer, the quick replies ranging from joking about looking forward to some excitement to anger over the cowardly actions toward a woman. Then he'd spoken with Leland, not giving him a chance to order Kurt to make other arrangements for her by telling him she stayed or he went with her. That had stifled the instant denial he'd seen as he'd spoken but not the flash of fear in his father's eyes.

"You'll be safe, and so will everyone else, Dad," he'd rushed to assure him. "You know how good our security is and have to know I wouldn't do this if I didn't think the risk to everyone was minimal and worth it."

Leland had shaken his head and turned away from him with a slump to his shoulders. "Fine. Just keep her out of my way."

Irritated, Kurt had snapped, "That won't be difficult since you rarely venture out of this room to be sociable to anyone."

Now, as he re-entered the quiet, darkened house, he breathed a sigh of relief Leland had turned in. He intended to rouse Leslie so she could eat something, but as he slipped into the guest room and spotted the empty plate next to the bed, he was relieved he wouldn't have to disturb her. Her eyes were clear the last time he checked on her and, according to Mitchell, it should be fine now to let her sleep.

He didn't like going to his room and leaving her to sleep alone but respected her wish to step back from the physical side of their relationship. After the obvious struggle she'd portrayed with wanting to keep him and others safe from whoever was after her, he didn't take that ultimatum personally. He also didn't intend to play fair in abiding by her wishes as soon as she healed enough to move around without pain.

To Kurt's surprise, he found Leslie already up, dressed and chatting with Babs in the kitchen early the next morning before he could introduce them. Sitting at the counter sipping coffee, she looked well-rested and not bad for someone who had survived such a horrendous car accident the day before. Gazing at the swelling and bruising around her bandaged head, his gut cramped with the same sucker punch as when he'd connected the dots between seeing the wrecked car and then Leslie on the ambulance gurney. He'd known in that moment of breath-robbing fear that sometime in the last month she had gotten under his skin too deep to let her go. For the first time in his life, he wanted a woman for the long haul and he embraced the prospect with a surge of protectiveness and excitement.

Now, all he needed to do was convince her to get on board with the idea.

"My two favorite ladies. Good morning." Strolling over to Leslie, Kurt watched her eyes widen in surprise and alarm as he bent to give her a thorough, deep kiss before drawing back and smiling at Babs. "I see you've met our guest."

Babs nodded, beaming at him. "She was telling me about what happened and trying to warn me to stay away from her outside the house." She huffed, stirring the pan full of fluffy eggs on the stove. "As if you or anyone else on this ranch would let anyone get close enough to harm her or me."

Leslie rolled her eyes. "Kurt can't be everywhere at once."

"No, but I can be where you are whenever you leave the house," he returned, walking over to get a cup of coffee. "How are you feeling this morning?"

"Sore but better. Thank you for setting the pain pills out for me. They helped enough last night and I don't need them this morning."

"Don't push yourself, Leslie. Do you remember what your car looked like?" He sure as hell did. It was something he doubted he would ever forget. Sliding onto the seat next to her, he eyed her askance, wondering how soon he could start poking at her for the whole story behind her placement in witness protection.

"I remember," she admitted with a visible shudder, tightening her hands around the coffee mug. "I guess I should be grateful he missed instead of killing me with a direct hit."

Cocking his head, Kurt regarded her solemnly before saying, "He didn't miss, sweetheart. Grayson speculated he aimed for the tire to drive you off the road and then for the gas tank, which he did miss, but not by much. An explosion would have delayed not only identifying you, but the car and discovering the bullets."

Her hands shook, forcing her to set down the cup. Rubbing her palms up and down her jean-clad thighs, she blew out a shaky breath. "I didn't think of that."

"Oh, honey, don't you fret." Babs set a plate of eggs in front of her and reached over to pat her forearm as Leslie brought her hand up from her lap. "Anyone would be a fool to try and come after you on Wilcox property. Eat your breakfast."

Kurt's lips curved at Leslie's bemused expression. "Don't argue with her, it won't do you any good."

She flicked him a sly, teasing glance. "Like with you?"

"Exactly. When you're done, you can write the things you

want from your apartment. Or would you rather go into Willow Springs when you feel up to it? We can purchase whatever you need for the next few weeks."

She shook her head and then winced, brushing her fingers over the bandaged bump above her right eye. "I don't want to answer any questions and I'm sure news of this has already made the small-town gossip circles. Besides, I'm not anxious to get back on that highway anytime soon."

"Then it's settled. I'll run into Billings and get your things this morning, while you're still recovering inside. It won't take me long. As soon as you're up to it, we'll start target practice."

That had her halting her fork halfway to her mouth as she paused to say, "Huh?"

He nudged her fork hand forward. "You heard me. It's past time you knew how to defend yourself. Gotta run so I can get back." Taking his plate to the sink, he asked Babs, "If Dad's plate is ready, I'll take it to him."

Leslie frowned. "Why doesn't he eat in here with us? You shouldn't cater to him. That just enables his bad behavior."

Kurt lifted an inquiring brow, regarding her with curiosity. "Have you met Leland?"

"Yes, last evening." She waved her hand holding the utensil. "It only took a few minutes to ascertain he could benefit from more blunt speaking. Sorry if I've overstepped, that's just my opinion."

"And here I thought I was the only one who had the guts not to put up with his bullshit."

"Language, Kurt," Babs admonished, swatting at his shoulder.

"Right." He winked at Leslie. "Go for it, sweetheart." He handed her Leland's plate. "I'll get out of here a lot faster if I don't see him first." Giving her another kiss, this time by tugging her head back with a handful of hair, he strode out with her narrowed-eyed glare drilling a hole in his back.

149

BJ WANE

LESLIE TURNED from watching Kurt walk out, her blood having pooled in a hot puddle between her legs and her nipples peaking in her usual response from his touch. She encountered Babs' knowing grin and returned it with a rueful smile. "Has he always packed such a wallop with the girls?"

Babs bobbed her head. "Oh, yes, ever since he was too young to know what those looks meant."

Leslie smirked. "I bet it didn't take him long to find out."

Babs turned serious. "No, but he also didn't let it go to his head and get all cocky like some teenagers. His father taught both Kurt and Brittany to respect others and hard work." Sadness flitted across her rounded face. "It was a shame, what happened to that girl, and what her passing did to the two of them."

She wanted to know the whole story, but it should come from Kurt or his father. Maybe helping them mend their rift would ease some of the guilt riding her over the unconditional stance of protection Kurt and his employees had given her. Eying the two plates Babs was filling with eggs, sausage and toast, she asked, "Who's the second one for?"

"Cory, Mr. Wilcox's aide. He'll be in there by now."

"Mind if I deliver them? I'd like to make myself useful."

Babs cast a critical eye over her before handing Leslie the plates and pointing in the opposite direction of her guest room. "The master bedroom is on the far south end of that hall. The missus wanted privacy from her children. Just don't overdo. I'll be here all morning, so you tell me if you need anything."

She grasped the plates, grateful for Babs' support. "I will, Babs. Thank you."

Leslie got a better idea of how the sprawling, one-story house was laid out as she wound her way toward Leland's quarters. Splashes of sunlight streaming through wide windows and

150

skylights brightened the buffed, dark hard wood floors through-out, the views outside them amazing, no matter what direction you looked. She itched to explore the property, get a closer look at the beautiful Thoroughbreds she spotted grazing in the pastures and familiarize herself with the running of a working ranch. In the three and a half years she'd lived in the midst of cattle country, she'd stuck to the familiarity of city life, but now found herself interested in learning more about how Kurt spent his days.

That new interest didn't bode well for keeping a physical distance between them, but she wouldn't be content to sit around the house all day for long. She needed to stay busy to keep from freaking out over someone intent on killing her.

The door stood open when she reached the bedroom, the frustrated voice coming from inside reaching her before she saw who it belonged to.

"Why don't you want to go this morning?"

"I didn't sleep well," Leland snapped.

A tall, young man in his mid-twenties shook his blond head at Kurt's father who was up and dressed and sitting at a small table in a corner of the spacious room. "You used that excuse last week."

Leslie held up the two plates as she entered. "Maybe break-fast will perk you up and then you'll feel like going out." She smiled at the aide. "Hi, I'm Leslie."

"Kurt mentioned you this morning. I'm Cory," he said, reaching for the plates. "Thanks but I could've gotten them."

"No problem." She looked down at Leland with a wry expression. "Are you starting the day giving him a hard time? I don't know you except for what Kurt's mentioned, but I'll bet you're balking at going into therapy again."

Leland's glare reminded her of Kurt's when he was annoyed with her. "Mind your own business," he returned sourly.

"I'd love to but your stubbornness is weighing your son down with worry and since I care about him, I hate to see him upset. I would think his father would have even stronger feelings." Satisfied with the consternation filling the older man's eyes, she beamed at Cory. "Nice to meet you. I'm going to rest so I don't give my generous host anything else to fret over."

Cory's face split in a knowing grin. "Nice to meet you, too."

Pivoting, she ignored Leland's disgruntled *hrrmph*. Her gaze landed on a chess set by the window as she headed out. An idea took hold and, pausing, she turned her head to say, "I used to be damned good at that game. I'll play a match with you after your next therapy session." Satisfied she'd given him something to think about with that challenge, she left the room.

Leslie made it back to her room, closed the door and leaned against it before her trembling body could threaten her composure. Admitting her feelings hadn't been easy and added to the hardship of her uncertain, risky future. It also ratcheted up her anger over her circumstances, Edwin Glascott and whoever he hired to come after her. Stuck between a rock and a hard place, she prayed for a quick, safe end to the threat against her, wondering if it was too much to hope she could stay in Montana and see where these feelings could lead.

KURT KEPT himself busy over the next few days, giving Leslie time to recover and think about where she wanted to go from here. Denying her submissive needs while living alone and staying home from the club was one thing, dismissing them while living with her Dom would be much harder. He joined her for dinner Monday night and breakfast the next morning, sitting close, touching her often, and enjoyed watching her tremble or hearing her sudden, indrawn breath, the flash of arousal in her eyes before she masked it with annoyance.

The unguarded moments when he caught the fear and

uncertainty on her face tore at him, her hands-off stipulation grating the most then, the depth of his feelings as obvious to him as the sun at high noon on a cloudless day.

Tuesday morning, he started the day on a positive note when Leland announced he was going into therapy. Kurt greeted the news with relief even though he silently questioned his father's change of heart. And then he'd returned to the house for lunch and found Leslie sitting with his father, her hand hovering above her bishop on the chess board that had gone unused since he'd returned. When his dad refused to join them in the kitchen for lunch, she'd surprised him by standing and saying, "Then we'll have to finish this later because I want to have lunch with Kurt in the kitchen." She'd breezed out with a small smile, his father's irritated scowl priceless.

And Kurt fell in love a little bit more.

Now, as he let Atlas out in a full run back to the stables two days later, Kurt realized Leslie had transferred her drive for encouraging kids to work hard toward reaching their full potential to his father. Whenever he saw her with Leland, sparring over a chess game with Cory looking on in bemusement, the clutch around his heart gripped his chest tighter. She'd even managed to coax Leland out to the patio table for dinner last night after Kurt grilled steaks for everyone, including Roy, Babs and Cory.

As pleased as he was with her efforts toward his father, Leland still kept a wall between him and Kurt, still refused to discuss what had driven Kurt away for so long and wouldn't put out the effort to do anything physical outside of his bedroom. But as he savored the hoof-pounding ride across the pastureland, the strength of Atlas' bunching muscles against his legs and the brisk air rushing by him, he shoved aside thoughts of his difficult parent and focused on his difficult guest. Leslie was moving without pain, hadn't taken the prescribed meds past the first twenty-four hours and he'd caught several fleeting longing glances aimed his way from those blue eyes. It was time to push his sub back where she belonged, under his sexual control.

Pulling up on the reins, he slowed the stallion by degrees until he cantered into the stable yard with a toss of his head. "Yeah, that's my boy." Kurt patted his sleek neck before dismounting and looping the reins around the fence rail. Powerful ripples ran under the soft pale fur as he tugged the saddle off. He intended to escort Leslie to the stables soon and was looking forward to her face when he showed her the surprise he'd been holding for her, but today they would start target practice.

"I take it you located our lost mama and her baby," Roy said, walking up to run a hand over Atlas' flank.

"Took most of the morning, but yes, we found the calf in a ravine and mama standing guard out past the north ridge. How they managed to get so far from the herd is beyond me, but Travis and Casey will bring them in with them later today and I'll get the vet out here tomorrow."

"Sounds good. I've been asked by several hands when they get to meet the pretty blonde."

Kurt cut him a sharp glance, his brows furrowed. "How do they know she's a blonde? Rumor?"

A smile creased his manager's weathered, lean face. "Nope. She's been on the porch with Leland for the last hour, playing chess. Relax, Kurt." Roy rushed to assure him. "There's been someone within feet of the porch at all times even though no one can get close enough to the house to get to her or take a shot without being detected first. That's why you brought her here."

"Yeah, I know." The tenseness went out of his muscles. He'd spoken with Grayson every day this week, asking for news, but so far no leads had turned up. The sheriff's frustration matched Kurt's. "I planned on giving her a tour this afternoon on our way to the target area. I'll make some introductions then."

"I'll let them know." Roy started to turn away then paused to say, "I wouldn't be too quick to turn this one loose like you have all the others."

"If the authorities can't free her of this threat I may not have a choice." And that thought ripped at his insides with sharp talons every time the possibility snuck into his head.

"Then let's hope they're successful."

As Kurt slapped Atlas' rump, urging him into the paddock to romp with the mares waiting for him, he turned his mind to pulling more information from Leslie, teaching her to defend herself and reminding her of how he could distract her from her troubles. He spotted her still sitting on the porch next to Leland as soon as he came around the stables. Tipping his Stetson down, he stalked across the lawn wishing his father would look as pleased when they were together as he appeared with Leslie. Since his return, Leland had either been withdrawn or argumentative, but at least he hadn't hurled blame for Brittany's death at him again. That small boon gave Kurt hope they could eventually find their way back to a decent relationship. Right now he had another relationship that needed attention.

"Who's winning this match?" he asked them as he came up the steps.

"Girl's a damn good player, and devious. Challenges me then blackmails me into accepting." Leland glared at Leslie, but there was a twinkle in his eyes Kurt hadn't seen in way too long.

Leslie shrugged, her bland expression unconcerned with the accusation or his father's peevish tone. "You don't have to accept. Cory offered to play with me."

"I don't pay him to play chess."

"No, you pay him to drive you into therapy and help you get stronger here at home," she returned, jumping a pawn and snatching up one of Leland's men.

"I'm going, aren't I?"

"Not without arguing," she shot back.

"I owe you for getting him there twice this week, regardless of his reluctance," Kurt stated, enjoying their banter. Not many people stood up to his dad. "You'll have to pause this match. Leslie and I have a date for target practice."

She whipped her head up. "We do?"

He loved the skepticism in her eyes. "I told you I would teach you to defend yourself while you're here. You've recovered enough to spend an hour or two on your feet." He held out his hand to her as he looked at Leland. "Dad, do you need me to get the door for you?"

Leland's gaze flicked toward the cemetery then quickly away again. "No, I'll sit out here for a while."

LESLIE REACHED for Kurt's hand, wondering if she was the only one who noticed the flashes of guilt Leland portrayed whenever he eyed his son approaching him. And then Kurt's firm, calloused grip closed around her hand, diverting her attention to the immediate frisson of pleasure that simple touch radiated up her arm, making her question whether this was a good idea. The struggle to keep her longing for him and his sexual control at bay these past few days was more difficult than she'd imagined. The threat, her new surroundings and his nearness coupled by those probing, dark-eyed gazes kept her tense and always on guard with coping with all three. As he pulled her up, the peek she got at his expression from under his hat gave her pause. She knew that intent, determined look very well.

"Where are we going?" she asked as he led her across the lawn, the cool breeze more noticeable away from the protection of the house.

"We have a target range well away from the livestock and cowhands but I want to take a few minutes to show you around the grounds, even though I don't want you wandering around without me." He pointed to the nearest ranch building. "We board our personal mounts in this first stable along with the Thoroughbreds we breed and sell."

Like the house, the stable sported walls of half brick and half white painted siding with black trim. The building was massive with wide double doors opened to reveal rows of neatly kept stalls. The heads of several regal equines hung out window openings along the outside as they walked by.

"I've seen them in the pasture. They're beautiful to watch." And much bigger this close up, she mused, reaching up to rub a hand over the soft muzzle of a dark sable mare.

"That's Annie. She's too spirited for you. Tomorrow, if you're up to it, I'll take you up with me on Atlas and give you a riding lesson in the pasture." Kurt shifted and pressed one hand against her butt, prodding her forward.

Leslie tried to ignore the distracting goosebumps his touch produced but that proved impossible as he squeezed one cheek before resting that hand on her hip and halting to introduce her to the three cowhands coming their way. Flicking him an annoyed scowl, she held out her hand to the young men who looked to be in their early twenties and greeted her with polite 'Nice to meet you, ma'ams' before getting back to their chores.

"Everyone is so polite," she stated, fighting back a grin as she watched Kurt's employees swaggering strides they all seemed to have in common.

"A combination of good upbringing and wanting to earn brownie points with the boss." Pointing to a much smaller barn, Kurt started that way, saying, "Over here we house the livestock in need of special attention or veterinary care."

A loud neigh resonated from the corral in between the two structures, snagging Leslie's attention. An angry looking horse that needed to put on weight tossed his head with a snort as he pranced back and forth along the rail, eyes glued toward them. 'What does he want?" she asked, looking up at Kurt.

Dipping into his pocket, he pulled out a sugar cube and

nudged her toward the paddock. "A treat. I rescued him from the dog food factory and have been using bribes to gain his trust. I became his best friend when he got his first taste of sugar. Stay back, he'll bite if you give him a chance."

Bemused, she watched as Kurt held his hand out, palm flat and the mustang nipped the cube without checking it out first, his large eyes glaring at her with mistrust. "I don't know a thing about horses, but can't understand how anyone can allow one to get into this condition. Even I know their ribs aren't supposed to be so pronounced."

"Seeing an animal so neglected tries the patience of conscientious ranchers and livestock owners. Unfortunately, we see it all too often. This guy," Kurt managed to pat the horse's rump as he trotted away, "doesn't trust me enough to saddle him yet, but he will. I haven't failed with a reluctant partner yet." He cast her a pointed look before dipping his head to nip the tender skin along the curve of her neck, the slight sting ricocheting down her body.

Exasperated as much with him and his teasing touches as with herself for responding, she glared at him as he pulled back and nudged her toward the small barn again. "You agreed to set aside our physical relationship while I'm here."

"No, I didn't. I agreed we wouldn't sleep together," he replied smoothly, reminding her Doms didn't always play fair, or nice.

Before she could retort to that ridiculous excuse, he hauled her against him and covered her mouth in a carnal kiss that sent a flow of bubbling heat from her lips to her toes. Just as she leaned into him, telling herself it couldn't hurt to succumb to this pleasure one time, he broke away, snatched her hand and started walking again. Leslie glared daggers at his broad back, resisting the urge to deliver a kick to that fine ass as she ran her tongue over her throbbing lip. They wound their way around two more outbuildings, both as large as the first, and she met several more employees. Each time they moved away from the introductions,

Kurt would prod her along with teasing pinches to her backside, hard enough her jeans were no barrier to the resulting throb.

Swearing under her breath, Leslie wrenched her hand from his. "Not funny, Kurt," she griped before looking over his shoulder and gasping at the large moose staring at them from the edge of the woods. "Oh, wow, that thing is *huge*."

Kurt pulled the pistol from his waistband, his gaze turning sharp as he eyed the animal. "Stand still a minute. Odds are he'll keep on going unless provoked."

"You wouldn't shoot it, would you?" Between his size and antlers spreading out several feet from his head, the moose was a daunting sight, but also magnificent. She hated to think of him getting hurt, or worse.

"I will if he charges, but like I said," he nodded toward the lumbering animal turning back into the trees, "they usually don't stick around." Grabbing her hand again, he pointed in the opposite direction of where the moose had gone. "Come on. Fun time is over since the day is getting away from us. I want to get a little practice in before the sun starts to go down."

A five-minute walk brought them to a small open field divided by a small island range draped with Ponderosa pines. At the base of the ridge sat stacks of hay bales with painted circular targets on the front. Leslie shivered as Kurt settled her in front of him, not sure if the goosebumps racing across her skin were from the chill in the air or the press of all those hard muscles against her softer frame.

"Cold?" he whispered in her ear before warming her by sinking his teeth onto her earlobe.

"A little. Aren't you?" She cursed the breathless catch in her voice. Damn it, she wasn't a simpering teen with her first boy, or even a newbie sub with her first Dom. She was supposed to be put out with him, wasn't she?

"No. Just remembering when I had you at the club is enough

to keep me warm. Did I ever mention how much I like those little whimpers you make when I'm tormenting you?"

Why hadn't she realized how devious he could be, she bemoaned as those scenes popped into her head? "No, and I don't appreciate you bringing it up now."

"Then it's time to get serious." He placed her right hand around the butt of the pistol and her left below it, the smooth wood handle of the weapon in her hand creating a sense of anxiety out of the blue. Shaking it off, she concentrated on his instructions. "You'll do better with a double grip for now. A pistol has a kick to it, but nothing like a rifle. I took the bullets out, so don't worry about it being loaded."

"Is this necessary? I'm uncomfortable with this thing." *And with you being so close.* Was that the reason for her sudden nerves about the gun, the twitchy anxiety that wasn't there when she'd first seen it tucked into his waistband?

"Yes, and you'll get used to it. I learned to shoot before I started school. When I was around five, I witnessed a puma attack on one of our hands and saw how fast and accurately my dad reacted."

"Was he okay, your employee?" She shuddered, remembering the sudden splatter of blood as a bullet entered Alessandro's head and the nausea that unforgettable scene conjured up for months afterward.

"Yes. A few stitches and he was back to work thanks to Dad's excellent marksmanship. Now, pay attention."

Leslie tried but between Kurt's nearness and the memory of walking into that fateful scene, it was difficult. With his help, she took aim and pulled the trigger several times, breathing a sigh of relief the easier it got with each empty click. And then her unease returned as he loaded the gun with bullets. She quaked inside as she took aim, not understanding why until she squeezed the trigger and the loud rapport thrust her back to that day almost four years ago, and the horrible murder she'd walked in on.

Alarm bells went off as Leslie stiffened against Kurt and her face bleached to snow white. Her slight body trembled under his hands and against his chest, her calm, steady breathing turning to desperate pants, her eyes going blank with fear. Snatching the gun from her hands, he tossed it on the ground, grabbed her shoulders and gave her a small shake, worry and anger gripping his throat.

"Leslie!" he snapped. "Look at me." It took another shake before her eyes cleared enough to recognize him, the soft whimper spilling from her bloodless lips cutting him to the quick. "I'm here, baby. No one can hurt you. No one can get to you, I promise." She sank against him, still shaking but with a return of color to her cheeks. Relief loosened the knot in his belly as he pulled her close. "There you go."

Kurt held her for several minutes, doing nothing but rub soothing strokes up and down her back, waiting for her breathing to calm until she lifted her head. He wasn't surprised to see a return of wariness reflected on her face.

"I'm sorry." Leslie pulled back, averting her gaze. "I don't know what came over me."

"Yes, you do." He refused to let her revert to shutting him out. They'd come too far to start taking steps backward. Bending, he picked up the pistol and returned it to his waistband before latching onto her elbow and starting back to the house. "Can you talk about it now the secret about your placement in witness protection is out?"

She hesitated and then capitulated with a sigh that got to Kurt on several levels. "I guess there's no reason to keep quiet, is there?" Her eyes traveled around the pasture. "It's so quiet out here, so peaceful. That was the first thing I noticed about Montana. Such a vast difference from Reno."

"That's where you're from?" Keeping his steps short and slow to give her time to gather her thoughts, he watched her face closely for signs of duress.

She nodded, still not looking at him. "Yes, born and raised. I loved shopping at a corner Italian market, a small quaint, family owned grocery you don't find in big cities anymore. Alessandro Carmichael always greeted me by name and tossed a handful of gran gelees citrus fruit candies into my bag at checkout." The aching fondness in Leslie's voice and devastation reflected in her now clear eyes threatened to tear a hole in Kurt's gut "They're orange and lemon flavored soft Italian candies that I used to crave." She released a wistful sigh before wiping all expression off her face. "I haven't had one since I saw two spoiled rich teens put a gun to his head for no other reason than drug-addled kicks."

Now it was his turn to shake inside in both fear for her and fury over everything she'd lost. He couldn't imagine the shock and trauma of witnessing such a thing. "Jesus, sweetheart, no wonder you freaked out at the sound of a gunshot. What happened? Did they get off and threaten you?"

"No, they just died in a prison fight. It's their father who threatened me after I testified and who we suspect is behind the attempted hit on me now. My liaison in the program informed me of a breach into their protected files not long ago. They're working on connecting all the dots."

The house came into view and he paused, turning her to look at him. "You don't trust they'll find proof to arrest this guy?"

"No, since they haven't done so in the last four years," she returned in a clipped tone, resignation on her face.

"Then it's a good thing you have me, isn't it?" Because he sure as hell wouldn't let anything happen to her. Kurt hadn't needed a mule to kick him in the head to force him to admit sometime within the last two weeks, his feelings had taken a dive off the deep end. Love left him no choice but to keep Leslie glued to his side for the next forty years or so.

Chapter 11

"Can I help you?" Alan strolled towards the man who appeared uncomfortable walking the hall of an elementary school after dismissal. With the exception of a few teachers and the office staff, the classrooms and halls stood empty.

"I hope so," he replied with a rueful smile. "I'm trying to find an old friend from college, Leslie Collins. I've been unable to get hold of her by phone to let her know I was coming through this way and she hasn't been home the two times I stopped by her place. The last time we spoke, which I admit has been awhile, she mentioned teaching here. I was hoping to catch her before I have to head out."

"Sorry." Alan shrugged. "She surprised everyone by taking a sudden leave of absence a few days ago for a family emergency." Even though Leslie had politely turned down his date invitations, he couldn't suppress his disappointment when she'd left without a word. He knew little to nothing about her other than she was an excellent teacher, the kids adored her and her smile always stirred up a warm, pleasant sensation inside him. The regret etched on the man's face mirrored his own when he realized her smile wouldn't brighten his days for an unknown time period.

"That's too bad. I hadn't heard that and I have to leave first thing in the morning."

It would be a shame if Leslie missed seeing an old friend and Alan could think of only one other person who might have more information to help him. "She's been seeing a man named Kurt Wilcox, a local rancher and large property owner. If you can find a way to get hold of him, he might know where she's at." As soon as he'd seen the possessiveness stamped on Wilcox's face that afternoon in the parking lot, Alan had accepted he didn't stand a chance with her. It didn't matter she hadn't appeared happy with whatever they were discussing; her body language spoke volumes in the way she leaned toward the other man, the flush on her face and look in her eyes she'd never bestowed upon him.

"Hey, thanks." He held out his hand to Alan, an expression of gratitude erasing the letdown on his face.

"Good luck."

As soon as Clayton Mahoney returned to his motel room, he opened his laptop and looked up the Wilcox Ranch, somehow not surprised to find its location within a few miles of where he'd ambushed his mark's car. His client's rage over his failure to take her out a few days ago had blistered his ear through the phone. Normally he would walk away from a job when the customer came across as unhinged, but the extra one hundred thousand he'd dangled in front of him on top of the quarter million already promised was too tempting to turn down.

Before calling in with this latest information, Clayton scouted out the ranch where he suspected the Collins woman was hiding out. After discovering the risk of breaking through the tight security at the front gates, he returned the next day to check out the perimeters of the seemingly never-ending acreage. It took him hours of non-conspicuous driving where he spotted rifle-toting men on horseback, driving trucks or riding ATVs, depending on the terrain they were patrolling, to conclude this wouldn't be an easy feat. Executing the job on a horse was out since he'd never ridden, and the trucks driven by the employees were all etched with the ranch logo, eliminating that option once he breached the security. But an ATV he could handle, and when he picked up a hat and covered his lower face with a bandana as he'd seen some do to keep the dust out of their mouths, anyone spotting him wouldn't know he was trespassing. Not until he'd completed the contract and was long gone, he hoped.

Picking up his phone, Clayton wasted no time relaying his news as soon as his employer answered. "I have a location where I suspect she's hiding. I'll need time to stake it out and verify while I research the best way to break through the security."

"Make it fast, damn it. I want the bitch gone," he barked without a hint of gratitude for Clayton's progress.

"Don't push me, Glascott." Dead silence greeted his knowledge of Glascott's identity. "Yeah, you son-of-a-bitch, I know who you are. It was worth spending a few thousand of my fee to have someone follow the money trail of my down payment, so do not fucking push me. I'll be in touch." He hung up, satisfied with the day's work.

KURT STRUGGLED to get the image of Leslie walking in on a murder out of his head but failed miserably. Waking the next morning after a long sleepless night, the first thing he did after dressing was check to see if she'd fared any better. Finding her in the kitchen making a stack of banana and nut pancakes, a cup of coffee within reach and swaying to whatever song was playing in her earplugs, he realized he needn't have worried.

She jumped when he snuck up behind her, gripped her hips and pulled her back against him. The hand flipping a pancake on the griddle stilled as she turned her head and glared at him.

Yanking out the earplugs, she grumbled, "You could've let me know you were there."

"I could have but this was more fun." Lowering his head, he nipped her earlobe and she shivered against him. "You're up early, and look well-rested. No problem sleeping after your flashback yesterday?"

She shook her head. "No, I've had plenty of time to learn to adjust when that memory pops up. I'm sorry if I freaked you out."

"You didn't, just caught me by surprise and I'm still working my way toward coping with what you went through." Sliding his hands upward, he watched her face as he skimmed his thumbs over her nipples, her light sweater and bra not enough to hide the instant pucker.

"In case you didn't notice, I'm still struggling with coping. I'm not sleeping with you, Kurt," she reminded him in a breathless rush.

"Not asking you to, sweetheart. When I'm touching you, sleeping is the last thing on my mind." Satisfied, he stepped back and moved to the opposite counter to pour a cup of coffee. Over his shoulder, he asked, "Why are you making breakfast? Babs leaves casseroles in the refrigerator for the weekend."

"I told her not to make one for breakfast. I need something to do and enjoy cooking when I have the time. Right now, I have too much time on my hands. I'm going stir crazy." She set a platter with a tall stack of golden brown pancakes on the table where he noticed three place settings. When she saw his questioning look, she sighed with a shake of her head. "I thought Leland would join us but he declined. He wasn't happy when I refused to bring him a plate."

"He's not happy no matter what anyone does," Kurt retorted as he took a seat. "But thanks for trying." Digging into the fluffy pancakes, he knew he needed to tell her more about Brittany's death, but opted to wait until he took her riding. Having a view of the wide-open prairies backed by the snow-capped mountains with the endless blue sky above him and a fresh breeze to stir his senses helped distract from the melancholy talking about his sister always produced.

"Since you've tabled our Dom/sub relationship, we'll stay home tonight from the club. Looking at your head, I'm guessing the rest of your bruises are in the same sickly greenish/yellow stage and still a little sore, so that's just as well, but are you up for a slow ride this afternoon?"

Leslie's eyes lit up, her desire for more activity outweighing any lingering discomfort from the accident. "I can be ready as soon as I clean up in here."

"I do love your enthusiasm, sweetheart. Damn, these are good."

"Thanks. My sister taught me how to cook and passed Mom's recipes down to me." A shadow darkened her eyes before she averted them. "I haven't made them in a while."

He poured more syrup over his fourth serving. "You haven't spoken to your sister since entering the program?"

"No. I was allowed to tell her I was entering it and say good-bye. She understood but I miss her."

He hated seeing a return of that desolate sadness on her face. "Then let's hope the Feds can find something on this guy soon. Come on. Let's finish and get going." With luck, his surprise followed by her first ride would perk her up.

Kurt helped her clear the table and then she shooed him out to finish by herself so he could check on his father before they left. It didn't surprise him to find Leland staring out his bedroom window. Taking a deep breath, he decided it was time to bring up why he'd separated himself from Leland and his home for so long. If he expected Leslie to open up about her past, he could do no less.

"Monday will be ten years."

Leland's shoulders went rigid at the reminder and Kurt

didn't need to see his face for proof he wasn't happy. "You don't have to tell me. I've suffered her loss every damn day since, without you or your mother around to help bear the grief."

"You can't blame me for that. I'm no more responsible for Mother's cancer than I was for Brittany's drug and alcohol abuse," he retorted. Bracing for a return of accusations, Kurt jolted when his father agreed.

"You're right, you weren't."

The relief rushing through his veins propelled him forward. "Well, that was a long time coming." He needed to speak with him face to face, but Leland held up a hand, halting his stride.

"Go on now. Weather is supposed to turn next week. Get your girl out while it's still doable."

That familiar implacable tone halted Kurt. He used that same inflection when he was determined to have his way. At least Leland had finally admitted he was wrong to blame him for his sister's behavior and death. That was a start, and something he'd all but given up hope of hearing. "There are pancakes in the kitchen. We won't be gone long." Not wanting to push his luck, Kurt left him alone to continue his silent vigil.

LESLIE WAITED for Kurt at the front door, glad to see he was still in a good mood following a visit with his father. She never knew when an argument would erupt between them.

"Where are we going?" she asked when he clasped her hand and led her toward the small barn instead of the corral where his horse stood watching him.

"Since you're wanting something to do, and feel up to moving around more, now's a good time to give you the gift I picked up a little while ago." Opening the door, he ushered her inside, the scent of hay and livestock hitting her nose, her curiosity changing to a giddy thrill when he stopped at the first stall.

Leslie had been waging a war against falling in love with Kurt since the night they met, and slowly failing. That was why, upon learning the accident was a deliberate attempt on her life, she'd pounced on that excuse to distance herself from him, at least physically. But as she gazed at the two poorly kept miniature horses from the auction, she lost another battle to keep her heart safe, and this time was in jeopardy of losing the war.

"They're yours, Leslie," Kurt said, opening the stall gate.

"But…" She reached out and petted the solid black one who nudged her hand. "I know nothing about how to care for them. And what if I have to leave?" The thought cramped her stomach. Staring at her with soulful eyes were two more reasons to stay.

Waving an impatient hand, he frowned and tightened his grip on hers. "We'll cross that bridge if we come to it. The vet has them on a special diet to put on weight. They're still too nervous to turn loose with other horses, but the guys get them outside every day for a few hours. You can take over that chore starting tomorrow. Come on, let's get going while the sun's high."

As soon as they exited the barn, she turned to him with a beaming smile of gratitude, unable to recall when a gift had meant so much. "Thank you. I don't know what I'll do with them, but I'll figure it out."

Leslie wasn't prepared for Kurt's jaw to tighten, or for him to yank her against him to ravish her mouth in a deep, tongue probing, possessively hard kiss right there in front of the ranch hands moving about with their chores. Unable to help herself, she sank against him, taking a moment to relish his unbreakable hold and the surge of aroused pleasure it ignited.

Kurt released her as abruptly as he'd hauled her against him, his dark eyes glittering with a look that left her as shaken as that kiss. She opened her mouth to say something, she wasn't sure what, but he pressed a finger over her throbbing lips. "Unless you're going to tell me you've changed your mind about tabling our relationship, keep quiet."

That firm, inexorable tone tugged at her nipples and produced a damp spasm between her suddenly weak legs, taking a chunk out of her resolve to keep him at arm's length. She nodded, not trusting her voice.

"That's what I thought. Let's go."

At least he shoved aside the irritation reflected on his face and in his voice by the time he saddled Atlas, swung up on the huge animal's back and leaned down with an outstretched hand to her. "Trust me, I won't let you fall."

Believing him, Leslie grasped his hand and found herself swung off the ground and plopped in front of him before she could take a deep breath. "*Oh!*" she gasped, daring to look down. Making a frantic grab for Kurt's arm, she jerked back.

Kurt chuckled and pulled her against him in a snug embrace as he steered the stallion out of the paddock. "Nice and slow. See, not so bad, is it?"

"No, not at this pace," she admitted, enjoying the sway of their bodies to the horse's steady movements. At least she didn't have to worry about the open air feeling cooler as they rode away from the protection of the buildings, not with the heat of Kurt's body spreading a slow warmth inside her. It was going to be a long ride.

He chuckled, the deep vibration in her ear popping up goose-bumps under her sweater and jeans. "Think about the other rides you like to take at a faster, rougher pace."

"Kurt…"

"Are you going to remind me you're not sleeping with me again?"

How could he annoy and amuse her at the same time? Unable to answer her own question, she said, "Why waste my breath?" and settled back against him to enjoy herself.

They rode at a sedate walk for thirty minutes, Kurt pointing out the woods he played in as a kid, the trails he rode with Caden and the areas where they used to gather to party as teens. Guiding Atlas through a large herd of black cattle, he stopped to talk to his hired hands, addressing each by name, and told her what physical condition they wait for the cattle to achieve before sending them to auction to get the highest price.

Kurt brought up his sister when they rode away from the others, relaying the sad tale of Brittany's death in a car accident as they traversed across the sweeping meadows blanketed with wildflowers and prairie grasses, bordered by forests of ponderosa pines, Douglas firs, spruce and aspen trees, the miles and miles of acreage broken up by an occasional island range. Her heart ached for the young girl who had turned in the wrong direction for help in coping with her mother's death.

"Eighteen is so young to lose a parent and twenty way too young to die. I am so sorry. Is that why you moved to Houston? To get away from the painful memories?" Having buried her mother when Leslie had still been in her teens, she could empathize with their grief.

"No, that decision had more to do with my dad laying the blame on me for failing to get Brittany under control."

The bitter sadness and underlying temper in his voice drew her head around, anger for the way Leland let his heartache get the better of him churning in her abdomen. "You know you did everything possible, don't you?"

An indefinable emotion entered his eyes as he squeezed her waist and said gruffly, "I do. And it helps Dad finally admitted he was wrong to do so." Kurt steered Atlas closer to the woods edge and Leslie caught the gurgling flow of a rushing stream coming through the trees. "I'll take you fishing in a few days and then grill our catch," he stated before turning Atlas around to start the trek back.

"Just don't expect me to touch, clean or debone the things," she replied, wrinkling her nose at the thought.

"You're such a city girl," he mocked, nudging the horse into a trot that jogged her against that hard frame.

His forearm muscles rippled under her hands as she clutched him, her mind shifting from slimy, flopping fish to the bulge her butt kept bouncing against. "Yes, I am," she admitted, her breath catching as he leaned down to whisper, "Hold on, sweetheart."

With a kick to his sides, the stallion took off, galloping at a speed that whipped her hair around her face, stole her breath and invigorated her senses. They sped by a shimmering lake, the deer getting a drink blurring along with the ground whizzing by below them. Leslie didn't know what produced the full body buzz enveloping her by the time Kurt slowed Atlas down – the wild ride or being nestled so close to Kurt again, his thick quads bunching against her hamstrings, his wide chest cradling her shoulders and the sure grip of his hands controlling the strong horse as easily as he had her after getting her naked.

Hours later, as she sank her sore body into a hot bath later that night, the draining, emotion packed day had her second-guessing her hasty decision to end their Dom/sub relationship. Leslie moaned as the heat and soothing water loosened her muscles, but admitted she could use Kurt's dominance right now to ease the tension of constantly questioning whether she'd made the right choices regarding the threat on her life.

KURT AWOKE Monday dreading the day ahead. Rolling out of bed after spending another night without Leslie's soft, naked body curled around him was only one of the reasons for his foul mood. Padding naked into the adjoining bath, he contemplated the merits and risks of yanking those tight jeans down, bending her over and spanking her ass until she begged for more and his frustration with her stubbornness abated. God knows he'd seen as much need for that action reflected in her eyes as he felt, and damn it, if something didn't break in her case soon, he would quit suppressing that urge.

Stepping in the shower, the second reason for his ill temper intruded on the enticing image of Leslie's reddened backside filling his head. He'd refused to come home on the anniversary of Brittany's death in the last eight years, but given his father's attitude since Kurt had returned, regardless of his acknowledgement Kurt wasn't to blame, he was bracing for Leland's mood to be as sour as when he'd driven Kurt away.

Funny, he mused as he lathered up. After knowing him less than two months, Leslie had turned to him the other day with confidence he'd done everything possible to help his sister after hearing the bare bones of his past. If he weren't already in love with her, the warmth of that unconditional support that obliterated the cold from his father's condemnation would have tipped the scales.

Kurt got dressed and headed into the kitchen, not surprised to see the vase of fresh flowers next to Brittany's picture in the den. Babs always remembered this day, as well as holidays and his sister's birthday.

"My two favorite girls," he said as soon as he saw Leslie standing at the griddle next to Babs. "What are you cooking up this morning?" He dropped a kiss on Leslie's head on his way to the coffee pot.

"Cinnamon rolls just came out of the oven and the eggs are about ready. Your dad refused to come out this morning." Babs sighed and Leslie frowned, casting him a concerned look.

"Didn't you expect that?" He squeezed Leslie's shoulder as he snatched a warm roll. "I'll take him a plate after I have a cup of coffee and eat this. I refuse to eat a cold breakfast to cater to him."

Roy came in just then and made himself at home grabbing a

plate and joining him, Leslie and Babs at the table. Having their silent support went a long way toward tempering his irritation and by the time he finished eating, he was in a somewhat better mood.

Tugging on Leslie's hair as he stood, he said, "As soon as I see to a few things, I'll return and take you riding again. I have a docile mare you'll like." Her eyes lit with pleasure and she leaned her head into his hand, a gesture lost on the other couple, but not on him.

"If you think I can handle riding solo, I'm game. I'll be ready when you are."

"That's my girl." Satisfied, he filled a plate for Leland and took a fortifying breath as he strode down the hall.

His father's strident voice reached him as he entered the master bedroom, dashing his hopes for another surprise change of heart today. "Don't argue, just cancel the damn appointment!"

"If that's what you want."

Cory's resigned disappointment stirred up Kurt's temper. Stalking across the room, he all but slammed the plate down on the small table, glaring at Leland who had turned from the window. "I'm assuming you're backing out of going in for therapy again."

"Don't start. You know what today is."

Kurt looked at Cory. "Go get breakfast. The people in the kitchen are preferable to this stubborn coot."

At least Leland waited until his aide left the room before rounding on Kurt. "You of all people should know how difficult today is," he snapped.

"Since you never let me forget it, yes. What does that have to do with you going to the clinic for therapy?"

"I'm not in the mood, and I told you I know you weren't to blame for anything," he returned with a stubborn set to his jaw.

"That was your excuse last week for skipping therapy, and

174

acknowledging your mistake is a good first step, but it's not enough, Dad." Crossing his arms, Kurt glared at him, refusing to back down. "I'm getting tired of pulling your weight around here. There are things you could be doing, and more things you would be capable of if you would put out a little effort."

"Fuck this God damned ranch!" he burst out, his face mottled with anger as he spun his chair around. "You have no idea what it's like to lose a child. It rips you up inside, leaves a hole nothing and no one can fill."

Bitterness roiled in Kurt's gut and rose in a nauseous ball to clog his throat. If it wasn't for Leslie, he would go pack and leave for good. All his efforts in running the ranch these past weeks meant nothing to Leland. Saying he wasn't enough to fill the gap in his life from Brittany's death hurt. Leland had lost Kurt for eight years, and yet he still refused to work his way back to standing by his side.

"Well, thanks for letting me know where I stand once and for all. Sit there and rot. I'm done with this." He pivoted and stormed out of the house, never seeing Leland's shocked face or the sympathetic dismay in Roy, Babs and Leslie's gazes as he stomped by.

Leslie glanced toward Cory, who sat at the counter. "How could he talk that way to his son?" she questioned after hearing the argument between Kurt and his dad. He dashed out so fast she barely caught the anger tightening Kurt's jaw that belied the despair swirling in his eyes, but it was enough to make her own heart ache for him. The need to go to him and ease his pain and show him she cared nearly overwhelmed her, forcing her to grip the counter edge to keep from chasing after him.

In that brief moment, when she realized her need to alleviate his pain overrode her desire to protect herself by keeping her distance, she tumbled the last drop into love, losing the war she'd been waging with herself since she'd taken his hand and accepted his help up from the sidewalk two months ago.

"I haven't been able to figure him out since I started working for him." Cory swallowed the last bite of cinnamon roll and rose. "I better get back in there and see what I can do."

"I would go with you, but I'm too pissed right now," Roy said, slapping his hat back on his head. "Stubborn doesn't begin to describe that man."

Babs blinked away the tears swimming in her eyes as Leslie started cleaning up. Twenty minutes later, as she dried her hands and glanced out the window above the sink, she spotted Cory walking back to the house from where he'd left Leland sitting inside the fenced family plot. Shoulders slumped, the older man appeared lost in dejection and her heart went out to him despite her pique over his treatment of Kurt.

"He was just as morose when Kurt lived in Houston," Babs said as she joined her at the window. "I really thought Leland would perk up once Kurt moved back."

Remembering the spasms of guilt Leslie had glimpsed crossing Leland's face that Kurt missed, Leslie harbored doubts as to the reason for his behavior. "*Mmmm*, I think I'll go sit with him for a while," she murmured.

Her first year in Montana, Leslie learned how early winter arrived and how long it lasted. Changing into a sweatshirt, she strolled across the wide lawn, grateful for the sun and lack of wind as the air carried a decided nip. The iron gate to the hilltop plot creaked as she opened it, drawing Leland's hopeful look around. His face fell when he spotted her before he smoothed out his features.

"I'd rather be alone," he stated with a dip of his brows.

"No you wouldn't." Taking a seat on the quaint garden bench next to his chair, she said baldly, "You've just backed yourself into a corner and now don't know how to get out of it."

"What are you talking about, girl?" He huffed in annoyance and slid his eyes back to the ornate headstones.

"I'm sorry for your loss, but that's no excuse to hurt your son."

And there it was, that quick flash of guilt that stripped the color from his lined face and caused the slump of his shoulders. Only this time, he didn't try to hide or erase his feelings.

"What I said this morning, it came out wrong and he misunderstood."

Leslie patted his leg, surprised to feel a firmer quad muscle than she'd expected. Another revelation he needed to account for. Later though. "If you're worried about losing him, or think you already have, why aren't you trying harder to get him back?"

Leland shook his head. "How can I ask him to forgive me for the way I lashed out at him after Brittany's death? Whenever I think about those times before he left, I can't imagine how I could do such a thing, or why he'd ever forgive me. I told him I no longer held him responsible, hoping that would be enough."

"Leland, you've been blinded by grief for so long, you can't see what's right in front of you." She pushed to her feet. "He came back every year just so you wouldn't have to spend the holidays alone. Upon hearing about your stroke, he dropped everything to rush to your side and then didn't hesitate to make immediate arrangements for returning and helping you out. How can you think he wouldn't let past hurts go in favor of having his father back?"

Pivoting, she made it to the gate before he called back to her. "You're a good girl, Leslie, and good for my boy."

"I just wish that was enough to keep me here," she said, thinking of her own problems.

Halfway across the yard, she hailed one of the hands exiting the large barn and asked him if he knew where she could find Kurt.

"Yes, ma'am." He pointed to the tack building between the stables. "He's been in there all morning. You take care now."

With a tip of his hat, he strolled off with a swagger that always tugged at her lips.

Veering toward the outbuilding, Leslie turned her mind toward being there for Kurt with as much support and caring as he'd given her.

Chapter 12

Leslie entered the shed, the leather odor filling her nostrils the same moment her eyes found Kurt across the room. She paused, her heart stuttering, stopping then hitching into overdrive as she took in his shirtless appearance. His arm muscles flexed, his broad back glistened with a light sheen of sweat despite the cool temperature, his black hair clinging damply to his corded neck. The heat emitting from the fire burning furnace next to him paled in comparison to the hot torrent of blood through her veins. Her nipples went hard, her pussy spasmed, and when he lifted his dark head, nailing her with those midnight eyes, her buttocks clenched. But more than the realization of how badly she ached to resume their physical relationship, she yearned to erase the haunted look reflected on his face.

"Go back to the house, Leslie. I'm busy."

Okay, he wasn't going to make this easy. Refusing to back down from his cold reception, she wound her way slowly toward him, maneuvering around saddles draped on top of sawhorses, past the wall of hanging leads, bridles and reins, a large bin of metal horseshoes and a few pieces of equipment she did not want to know what they were used for.

His forearms and biceps rippled as he worked an oiled cloth over the seat of a saddle. "What are you doing there?"

Looking up, Kurt's eyes flashed and his shadowed jaw tightened. God, she loved that stern, dominant stare, the one that said she was pushing her luck and gave her goosebumps. An idea formed, a risky, heart thumping thought that turned her palms as damp as her pussy.

"Working, and now wondering why you aren't obeying me," he bit off. "I'm busy, as you can see, and don't have time to entertain you right now."

Leslie fought back her own retort, recognizing his need to protect himself, and her from the anger and pain his father's words wrought. The futility of trying to shield her heart by denying the strong physical needs he'd proven so good at satisfying was never so apparent, and she refused to back away from him again.

Lifting a hand to the buttons running from the scooped neckline of her thermal top to just below her breasts, she popped the top one free, lowering her other hand to the saddle between them. Running a finger over the smooth, warm leather, she said, "Funny, you've been wanting to entertain me since I got here. Tell me why you're rubbing that nasty smelling stuff onto your saddle." Her eyes lifted from his hands to his face as she flipped open another button.

"You're playing with fire, sweetheart. Knock it off," he warned.

"It's hot in here." Opening another button, she sidled over to a rack and pointed to what looked like a branding iron. "You don't use that on your livestock, do you?" she asked with a shudder of revulsion.

"Sometimes, depending on the animal and the need."

She turned back to him, freeing the last button. "That seems cruel."

"It's not," he retorted. Cocking his head, he regarded her with a calmer expression that ratcheted her arousal another notch, and conjured a frisson of trepidation as only a Dom's pointed look could. "I thought you didn't want to sleep with me."

"I don't want to sleep." Releasing the front hook of her bra, she pushed the top and loose cups to the side and palmed her left breast. Rasping her thumb over the turgid tip, she sucked in a breath as she baldly stated, "And I've changed my mind about stopping our physical relationship."

Kurt's face didn't soften as she'd hoped, nor did those black eyes reveal pleasure at her announcement. Refusing to give up, she shoved aside her submissive voice reminding her of the repercussions of pushing a Dom too far and forged ahead, willing to risk just about anything to erase the hurt his father caused. "In fact, I'm ready to pick up where we left off right away." Stepping over to him, she continued to play with her breast as she cupped her free hand over his rigid, denim-covered cock. "See, you are pleased with my change of heart."

"That doesn't mean I appreciate you interrupting me, disregarding my order to leave, or touching yourself without my permission."

"Oh, my, I've really racked them up, haven't I?" Leslie shivered with the endless possibilities of his retribution, already feeling the heat blossoming across her backside. Dropping to her knees, she gazed up at him as she unbuckled his belt and slowly lowered his zipper. "Since I'm already in trouble, I may as well go for what I want." The hot, heavy weight of his erection fell into her hand, the pearl of moisture beaded on the smooth cockhead too tempting to resist. Ignoring the way his eyes went to black slits and the almost painful grip of his hands in her hair, she filled her mouth with his steely cock.

"Son-of-a-bitch," Kurt swore as she swirled her tongue under the plum shaped rim, teasing that sensitive spot before stroking downward, the thick, pumping veins jumping under her tongue.

Leslie relished his taste as much as his response and tight hold of her head by her hair. How had she managed to deny herself the pleasure of him? Maybe admitting how deeply her feelings ran had helped prod her toward taking this step, but she figured the biggest factor was wanting to ease his pain while storing up as many memories as possible to take with her if she was forced to leave. Either way, at this moment, here was where she wanted to be, where she needed to be.

Despite his sour mood, Kurt's cock twitched, engorging and heating more and more with every lick of Leslie's tongue, each nip of her teeth and the low moan erupting from her throat to vibrate against his flesh. He hadn't wanted company right now, not while he was struggling to find a reason to continue living under the same roof as his father. The thought of returning to Houston was as appealing as holding himself back from his sub these past ten days, and he couldn't bring himself to leave his home again.

Watching her face flush as she'd fondled herself had been Kurt's undoing. A Dom could only hold back for so long, and no one could expect a man denied the one woman he craved above everyone else to keep himself in check when faced with such an offer. While he appreciated her support and efforts to boost his spirits, as well as the pleasure her hot mouth was delivering, his mood wouldn't allow for her deliberate disobedience to go unaddressed.

Gritting his teeth, he pulled back from the wet suctions of her mouth, yanking on her hair as she tightened those soft lips around his cockhead and laved the seeping slit, her hands gripping his thighs. "As good as that feels, sweetheart," he rasped, "it won't get you a reprieve." Pulling on his control, he stepped back and hauled her to her feet, making short work of loosening her jeans and tugging them down. "You should have left when I told you. Now your only recourse is to say red." Spinning her around to face the propped saddle behind her, he tugged the shoulders of her top and bra down to her elbows, trapping her arms at her sides. "Bend over," he commanded, applying pressure between her shoulders until she lay belly down on the saddle.

Leslie lifted her dangling, flushed face to say, "I won't need my safeword," and then looked back down at the wood floor.

The work going on around the stable yard seeped through the thin walls of the tack shed, but as Kurt swatted her upturned ass, he doubted the bare-skinned smacks reached the ears of any of his cowhands. As her soft, malleable flesh warmed under his palm, he decided he didn't care if he was wrong. With each slap, her buttocks bounced and her breathing hitched. He delivered a string of steady spanks that covered her entire backside and then added strength to the last few aimed at her tender sit-spots. By the time he administered two more blistering blows, one in the center of each buttock, the delicate pink hue had deepened to dark crimson, her mewling whimper accompanying the uncomfortable shift of her hips.

Running his hand over the abused skin, Kurt stated, "That ends your warm-up."

Whipping her head up and around, he almost smiled at her startled look. "Warm-up?" she squeaked.

"You didn't think I'd let you off that lightly, did you?" He could feel her wide blue eyes tracking his movements as he stepped over to the wall and removed one of the narrow short leads. "This should do."

"Uh, Sir, maybe we could talk about this." Leslie's face had paled but arousal still shone in her eyes and glistened along her slit.

"Maybe *you* should have thought of the consequences before defying a direct order."

"I was only trying to…"

Kurt snapped the lead across her butt, snagging her breath.

"I know what you were doing, and why. But, as much as I appreciate your intentions, only my father can mend things between us. Say your safeword or turn around and be quiet."

"Fine." She huffed, flipped her head back down and wiggled her ass, a gesture that both amused and aroused him.

Kurt wasn't as put out about her reasons for ignoring his wishes as he let on. Delivering a few strikes that wrapped the thin leather across both cheeks, he admitted to the satisfaction of seeing how much his girl cared. That didn't negate his annoyance over her refusal to leave him alone to stew in his bad mood. Still, he wasn't an unfeeling Master, and his cock was demanding relief too long denied.

He halted at five strokes, the red, puffy lines on top of the scarlet hue covering her ass enough to appease him. "You've tolerated your punishment very well, sweetheart." Cupping her puffy labia, he rubbed his palm up and down her damp seam.

Leslie groaned, pressing against his hand. She tried to move her arms and he heard her frustration as she realized the shirt still kept them pinned at her sides. "Sir, please," she whispered, the needy ache in her voice matching the throbbing demand of his cock.

"I've missed hearing you beg, sweetheart." Sliding two fingers deep inside her quivering pussy, he fished a condom out of his back pocket.

Hearing the rip of the crinkling wrapper, she turned amused eyes up to him. "You walk around your ranch with a condom in your pocket?"

"Only since bringing you here. Fuck but you're tight, and wet." Pulling his fingers from her grasping, slick heat, Kurt covered himself and slid inside her in one smooth stroke. "This is going to be hard and fast. Brace yourself."

She did so without complaint, grabbing the handle under the wooden sawhorse to hold on to as he pummeled her sheath with pounding thrusts. The stand wobbled under his assault but her weight, combined with the heavy saddle, ensured it wouldn't topple over. Just to be safe, he leaned forward, bracing his hands next to her hips, adding pressure as he used his line-dancing hip action skill to bury himself inside her over and over.

"That's it, Leslie," he ground out as those strong, velvet soft muscles clamped around his pistoning shaft then massaged his length with rhythmic convulsions. "Come on my cock, show me how much getting down and dirty with me in a shed turns you on."

At the club, she wasn't shy – few were after attending several times. But Leslie wasn't one to take risks, and that she would brave being heard by his hands, or someone walking in on them, told him how much she cared.

Convulsing around his ramming strokes, her cries of, "Yes, yes, *yes!*" resonated around the room as she exploded in climax.

Kurt shook and swore as her pussy kneaded his flesh until he saw stars from his own eruption, an orgasm that released enough endorphins to forget all about hurtful words. He continued to pump inside her as they both came down from the exultant highs by slow degrees, their harsh breathing echoing in the otherwise silent space.

"The next time you deprive me of your delectable body, I won't be so forgiving." He pulled back, helped her up and turned her to see her wide smile of satisfaction and mirth.

"If you call that spanking forgiving, I don't think I'll test that threat any time soon." Leslie leaned against him, rubbing her pointed nipples against his bare chest. "I've missed this, too."

Slapping her butt, he grinned. "Your fault." Kurt adjusted her top, latched her bra after licking over each nipple and then buttoned her up. "You right your jeans while I take care of myself, and then get out of here. As it is, our ride will have to wait until tomorrow."

Pulling up her jeans, she gave him a finger wave and sassy grin. "I liked that ride better anyway."

"LESLIE, LET'S GET GOING!"

Giving each miniature horse one last stroke down their nose, Leslie heeded the warning in Kurt's voice and backed out of the stall. She was already attached to the pair who watched her every movement with wide, wary gazes that tugged at her heartstrings.

"Coming, coming," she called out, rushing outside, squinting against the early afternoon sunlight.

She'd been disappointed when Leland didn't clear the air between him and Kurt yesterday, but was too relaxed from the night she'd spent in Kurt's bed and excited about riding the pretty mare he was leading toward her to worry about it. It was difficult enough to keep from fretting over the disruption of her life and the possibility of getting uprooted yet again. Both Agent Summers and Detective Reynolds had kept in touch and the latest news of a possible lead connecting a money trail from Glascott to a known thug with a long record offered the first sliver of hope.

"*Oh.*" Stumbling to a halt, Leslie held out a hand to the velvety soft nose reaching for her. The mare's charcoal brown coat and splash of white with chocolate spots covering the hind quarters gave away the breed. "She's gorgeous. An Appaloosa, right?"

Kurt nodded. "Yes, this is Anna Leigh, a new acquisition but I've ridden her to make sure of her temperament before picking her for you. She won't give you any trouble, and I'll ride as close to you as I can in case you get nervous. Ready?"

Leslie beamed at him, pleased to see his mood had improved from yesterday. "Ready." He boosted her up and as comfortable as she felt sitting astride the dainty mare, she missed all those hard, rippling muscles embracing her from behind. She had it bad for Master Kurt, she knew that now and didn't shy away from admitting it to herself. If only the threat against her would just go away, she could get more excited about seeing where this could lead.

"Good girl. Sit tight while I mount." Untying Atlas from the rail, he swung up on his massive stallion with an agility Leslie wondered if she'd ever achieve.

"So, where are we riding today?" she asked as they set out toward the east.

"I'm taking you around our lake. With luck, we might see an elk or a few of our bison. You look good, sweetheart. Not nervous?"

Kurt eyed her with those dark eyes and she was sure the nerves that look stirred up weren't what he was talking about. "No, not as long as we keep it to a walk."

"We can do that. It'll take us a lot longer, but we have a few hours before the temperature drops. Tell me more about your life in Reno."

CLAYTON MAHONEY HUNKERED down as he worked to disarm the security system along a line fencing where there were no visible cowpokes riding around. He'd taken two days to scout as much of the perimeters of the Wilcox spread as he could without drawing notice, but, fuck, their land went on and on and on. It was a good thing luck was on his side when he'd spotted his prey through the high-powered binoculars he'd forked out a wad for. The big man she rode with had given him pause, but if he was forced to take them both out then so be it. That extra hundred grand Glascott bribed him with was too damn tempting to back out now.

Disabling the alarm wouldn't be a problem, he figured, but not knowing if there was a back-up system that would send out an alert was an issue. He'd picked a spot as close to the house as he dared, hoping to catch her if she rode out again today.

All he had to do was hop on the ATV he already unloaded from the back of the truck he rented and drive around until he spotted her. As soon as he could get a shot off, he could be back at the truck and speeding away before anyone was the wiser.

Working on optimism, he took a deep breath and snipped the last few connections wiring an alarm along this section of fencing. Wasting no time, he pulled up the bandana to cover his lower face, adjusted his hat and drove the ATV through the gate, pushing it shut behind him before taking off.

"Damn, I'm good," he boasted aloud less than five minutes later when he lifted his binoculars and verified the woman riding alongside the same man was his contract. He was still too far away to get off a shot, but it wouldn't take long to cover enough distance to close the gap. Riding high on his anticipated success, he put the idling all-terrain vehicle in gear and sped across the prairie field, staying as close to a herd of cattle as he dared to aid in his cover.

AN ITCH between Kurt's shoulder blades warned him first, just seconds before his phone beeped with the security breach alarm code that went out automatically to every employee on the ranch. He should've known the day and his relationship with Leslie was going too well. Fury and gut-clenching fear rolled through his tense body as he pulled his rifle out of the scabbard and pointed toward the woods several yards away.

"Head that way, now!" he commanded, glad Leslie didn't hesitate. Keeping glued to her side, he checked the message, his alarm escalating as he read how close they were to the downed security line.

Leslie cast him a frantic look, her hands gripping the reins, her face draining of color as Kurt slapped the mare into a tro

"What's wrong?" she gasped, swiveling her head around, searching for trouble.

"Security's down…" Kurt swore as he saw the ATV and the driver aiming a gun their way too late. He yanked on the reins as the gun rapport echoed in the air. Atlas reared with a high-pitched neigh of pain as the bullet skimmed his flank, but obeyed his sharp commands of control. Lifting his rifle, he let loose with three rounds then jumped across the mounts to grab Leslie and throw them both to the ground on the other side of Anna Leigh, rolling fast to keep them away from the horse's pounding hooves.

Other than a soft startled cry as they hit the ground, she kept quiet, her slender body quaking under his as he said harshly, "Stay down, crawl into the woods and get behind a tree. Move!"

Kurt followed her, firing two more shots as he shouted to his stallion, "Atlas, home!" He breathed a sigh of relief as both horses took off back toward the stables as he reached the temporary safety of cover in the trees with Leslie.

"Now what?" she asked, her voice shaky as she gripped his forearm.

"Now we wait for backup."

MAHONEY CURSED and did a mental calculation of how long he dared try to pick them off before hightailing it out of here. No more than five minutes, and then he was gone. Staying behind the ATV, he peered through the binoculars and caught a glimpse of them inside the woods. Now, if one would just inch out enough, he could end this and be on his way.

LELAND, Roy and Cory were sitting on the front porch when the alarm came in. Within seconds, every cowhand working around the stables was rushing toward trucks or horses, the drills they bemoaned practicing every other month paying off.

"Sit tight. I'll be right back," Roy said, jumping up and shouting orders as he sent the men off in different directions.

"Where's Kurt?" Leland tried not to panic as he cast a wild look around the bustling yard for his son. Before Cory could answer, he watched in alarm as Atlas and another horse came barreling in from the pasture, icy tentacles of fear squeezing his chest when he saw the bright red splotch on the stallion's flank.

Fighting back the panic welling inside him, he called out to Roy who was sprinting toward the truck parked in front of the house. "Get the passenger door open. I'm going with you." Turning to Cory, he snapped, "Give me your arm."

Puzzled, Cory held out his arm, surprise spreading across his and Roy's faces as Leland stood showing more strength in his left arm and leg than they'd witnessed before.

Leland didn't spare them time for explanations. "Quit gaping and help me down the steps."

"You've been holding out on us," Cory accused, assisting him down the steps and over to the passenger side of the truck. "Why?"

"Not now. My boy is in trouble, and by God, I'm not sitting on my ass while everyone else runs to help him."

Enlightenment dawned on his employees' faces at the same time as Leland maneuvered with little effort onto the seat. But it was Roy who said, "You kept your progress quiet and fought against therapy to keep Kurt here, didn't you?"

"Talk later, drive now," he ground out, impatience snapping at his heels. Cory shut the door as Roy dashed to the driver's side and slammed the truck into gear.

Casting his friend and employer a disbelieving glance as he sped east, Roy muttered, "Why the hell didn't you just ask him to stay?"

Guilt settled like a heavy weight on Leland's chest, his eye shifting out the window at the land he loved so much. "I couldn't, not after the way I turned on him when we lost Brittany."

"You were grieving, Leland. The injustice of losing two family members so close together would drive anyone into lashing out at those around him."

"No, it wouldn't. Kurt would never behave in such a callous manner. Losing my wife, hell yes, that was hard, but a child, Roy, that's a kick in the gut you can't imagine. I'll be damned if I lose my son too."

GREED ENDED up costing Malone everything. Giving up after ten minutes, he started to crawl back onto the ATV only to see a cloud of dust hailing the arrival of multiple trucks and horseback riders converging on him. He was so fucked, he groaned, seeing the hard, grim faces staring at him, the number of guns leveled his way, but he aimed to get some satisfaction before going down.

"HOW'D they get here so fast?" Leslie took a deep breath of relief as she heard and then saw the cavalry coming to their rescue. Less than fifteen minutes had passed since those first shots had threatened her life and her sanity.

"Like I told you, sweetheart, you're safe with me. Don't move. They have him penned in between them and us. He'd be a fool to try anything now, but he might be desperate enough to prefer going down in a fight."

Another truck roared up, slamming to a stop in front of the semicircle of vehicles and horses, all of the cowhands aiming rifles at the lone assailant still squatting behind his ATV. Kurt almost fell over when his father slid out of the passenger seat and lifted his rifle above the door.

"Drop it you motherfucker," Leland ordered, his voice strong and sure, vibrating with a rage Kurt had never heard before.

"What the hell?" he muttered, confused and yet pleased beyond measure.

Despite the still dicey situation they were in, Leslie giggled, leaning into him. "He loves you, he just hasn't known how to ask for your forgiveness."

"But... *shit*!" Kurt lifted his rifle as their attacker stood and took aim their way, this time looking through binoculars at the same time. Before he could get off a shot, Leland beat him to it, his bullet hitting the man in the shoulder with enough force to drop him. A grin split his face as he grabbed Leslie's hand and led her out from behind the tree. "That's my dad. Come on, let's go home."

WORD TRAVELED fast and by the time they returned to the house, Grayson and his deputies were arriving with sirens blaring, the county ambulance right behind them. After loading his prisoner into the ambulance along with a deputy, the sheriff spent the next hour taking statements from everyone and calling the Feds with an update. The vet arrived to tend Atlas' wound, which only needed a few stitches and an antibiotic shot, much to Kurt and Leslie's relief.

As the cowhands started to disperse and return to their chores, Babs stepped onto the porch and announced sloppy joes and corn on the cob for everyone in two hours, a loud cheer greeting her offer. "Let me help," Leslie insisted, following Babs back into the house. After giving her brief statement that matched Kurt's to Grayson, she had needed to get out of the testosterone filled den and it had been nice to sit outside without worry. The inner shakes that had begun the moment Kurt had thrown her off Anna Leigh and that gunshot had tossed her back into the nightmare of walking in on Alessandro's murder were starting to subside. Now, all that was left to contend with was anxiety over the future. Just because one culprit had been taken out didn't mean another wouldn't follow.

They made a good team, Leslie thought, working with Babs to brown hamburger and fill buns with the barbequed meat. A long table was set up out front and the simple meal was devoured in no time, the camaraderie among the hands evident in the way they joked around as if nothing untoward had occurred that afternoon. Here less than two weeks, and Leslie realized how much she would miss them, the ranch, and even Leland if she couldn't stay.

"What's wrong?" Babs asked, giving her a one-arm hug as they stood side-by-side at the counter cleaning up several hours later. The sun no longer shone through the window and the gray evening cast of twilight mirrored her bleak mood. "Bad guy has been hauled off and everyone is safe, fed and happy."

"Yes, this time, but what about the next time? I can't stay here and risk everyone's safety forever."

"You won't be." Kurt strode into the kitchen, hauling her against him and kissing her with his usual deep possessiveness that she welcomed with a rush of heat. "I needed that. Been a hell of a day."

"What did you mean?" she asked, licking her lips.

Reaching for the last brownie sitting on a platter, he replied, "If you'd answer your phone, you would know. Edwin Glascott, that albatross around your neck for the last four years, committed suicide, apparently after hearing his hired thug was singing like a canary. You're free of him, sweetheart, and free to live openly wherever you want."

"I am?" she squeaked, thrilled beyond measure and yet saddened by another death as Kurt dragged her out of the kitchen.

"You are. Now," he stated, leading her onto the front porch, "all you have to decide is whether you love me enough to stay here with me, or if you need more time and want to return to your apartment."

Giddy with relief and pleasure, she flipped him a look of curiosity as he sat down and pulled her onto his lap. "Isn't returning to Reno one of my options?"

"No. There's nothing left for you there. Everything you want is here, and now yours for the taking. All you have to do is say yes." Gripping her hands together, he held them at the wrist as he bent and nipped at her neck before sliding his lips up to her ear. "I love you, Leslie. Is there really anything left for you to think about?"

"Well," she breathed with a catch as he flicked a nipple and she responded with a flood of liquid heat, "when you put it that way, no, there's not, Sir. Yes, I'll stay."

"That's my girl."

KURT LEFT LESLIE soaking in his big bathtub, intending to join her as soon as he wrapped up one more loose end to the day. He found his father in the den, sitting in his favorite recliner, a walker next to him, gazing at Brittany's picture. How could he have not seen Leland's ruse before now?

"Did you really think I couldn't forgive you for lashing out?" he asked, taking a seat on the sofa next to his chair.

"I would have had trouble, if the situation had been reversed." Leland slid his gaze from his deceased daughter to the son he'd come too close to losing. "But I should have tried. I'm sorry, Kurt. Once you came back, all I could think about was how to keep you here. I feared if I got back on my feet too soon you would return to Houston, and I would lose my chance to slowly make amends." He sighed, shaking his head at his own culpability. "Brittany was spoiled, you know that. You were nin when we found out we were going to have another child, and it was such unexpected and wonderful news. When her behavior turned wild in her teens, it was only her close relationship with your mother that kept her in check, I know that now. Without her, Brittany lost her way."

"We tried, Dad, both of us." Kurt saw the pain reflected in his father's eyes and his heart went out to him.

"No." He shook his head. "I didn't, not near enough. I laid it all on you because I couldn't get past my own grief. You were right to leave."

Eager to get back to Leslie, Kurt stood and reached out to squeeze his dad's hand. "We're good, Dad. I'm not leaving again, you're going to quit hiding your progress and push it even more now, and with luck, you'll be a grandfather by this time next year."

With that thought in mind, Kurt left Leland staring after him with tears swimming in his eyes and walked toward a future he never dreamed would be his.

The End

BJ Wane

I live in the Midwest with my husband and our two dogs, a Poodle/Pyrenees mix and an Irish Water Spaniel. I love dogs, spending time with my daughter, babysitting her two dogs, reading and working puzzles. We have traveled extensively throughout the states, Canada and just once overseas, but I much prefer being a homebody. I worked for a while writing articles for a local magazine but soon found my interest in writing for myself peaking. My first book was strictly spanking erotica, but I slowly evolved to writing erotic romance with an emphasis on spanking. I love hearing from readers and can be reached here: bjwane@cox.net.

Recent accolades include: 5 star, Top Pick review from The Romance Reviews for *Blindsided*, 5 star review from Long & Short Reviews for Hannah & The Dom Next Door, which was also voted Erotic Romance of the Month on LASR, and my most recent title, Her Master At Last, took two spots on top 100 lists in BDSM erotica and Romantic erotica in less than a week!

Visit her Facebook page
https://www.facebook.com/bj.wane
Visit her blog here
bjwane.blogspot.com

Don't miss these exciting titles by BJ Wane and Blushing Books!

Single Titles
Claiming Mia

AudioBooks
Bound and Saved

Connect with BJ Wane
bjwane.blogspot.com

Blushing Books

Blushing Books is one of the oldest eBook publishers on the web. We've been running websites that publish spanking and **BDSM** related romance and erotica since 1999, and we have been selling eBooks since 2003. We hope you'll check out our hundreds of offerings at http://www.blushingbooks.com.

CPSIA information can be obtained
at www.ICGtesting.com
Printed in the USA
LVHW051000220620
658650LV00006B/488